Ghosts, Gunman and the Grinning Cat

by

Malynda McCarrick

Malynda McCarrick

****Chapter One****

It looked like she was going to meet the Hunk-In-Room-2H sooner than she'd expected. Not that she cared. It wasn't like she'd be checking him out, not like she was interested. She had a strict rule about getting involved with hotel guests.

Never.

Not. Ever.

That didn't mean she couldn't enjoy the view. She could control herself, she was a grown woman, for gosh sakes!

With toolbox in hand, Danielle Jacobs made the climb to the second floor. Though Roxanna had told her to let herself in, she knocked before entering just to be safe. She knew where the problem was. She'd meant to fix it before anyone could use the room but this last minute room reservation moved up that schedule, so here she was making late night repairs to a pipe that would have been replaced next week. Unexpected repairs were just a part of doing business. Letting them sneak up on her normally organized and detail-oriented world was something she'd label as a never-let-it-happen-again moment.

The sound of dripping water led her to the kitchen area of the one bedroom apartment. She couldn't blame the new guest for requesting the repair, she wouldn't have been able to tolerate the steady drumbeat of a leaky pipe either.

Drip, drip, drip.

No, it had to be fixed now.

Crawling in under the cupboard on her back, she settled herself as comfortably as possible beneath the sink, organizing her tools within reach and got to work.

The noise woke him.

He'd been sleeping comfortably, dreaming of being home in his own bed in his rented condo in Chicago, when the racket in the other room told him the hotel repair man was probably fixing that dripping pipe. Two days of no sleep and several hours on the road had landed him here, yearning for a good solid night of sleep. One night, that's all it would take, and he'd be back to himself again.

Peace and quiet.

His agent thought peace and quiet was what he was looking for. Personally, he'd rather be back in Chicago, sharing a beer with friends in his favorite sports bar and enjoying the nighttime voice of the city. He preferred the noise and activity of big city life to the peace and quiet in God-knows-where, Iowa. Unfortunately, a book contract with a looming deadline and an impatient agent had placed him here...for now.

Since he wasn't going to get any sleep with all that noise going on, Eli Garrison rolled out of bed and shuffled into the kitchen in nothing but his silk boxer shorts.

All he could see through his weary eyes was a skinny overall-clad body hanging out from under the sink. He stepped over the guy on his way to the refrigerator, snagged a bottle of water, took a long gulp, and returned it to the refrigerator. As he passed the sink, he noticed it had grown quiet. "Hey, thanks for coming so soon to take care of that. If you don't need anything from me, I'll just head on back to bed."

He didn't wait for a reply.

He just wanted to crawl back in bed before the sheets cooled, hoping he'd find sleep again soon.

From under the sink, Danielle tried to concentrate as muscular legs clad only in boxer shorts stepped over her. With shaky hands she struggled to grip the wrench, trying not to drop it as she tightened the connection on the pipe, nervous sweat making the task more difficult than it should have been. Hearing his muttered words as he passed by a second time, she couldn't manage anything more than a strangled grunt then watch as those tanned, luscious legs carried him out of her sight.

The tight, strangling feeling in her chest told her she'd been holding her breath so she let it out with a whoosh. She hadn't even met the man and her body was fighting to maintain its normal functions, her heart couldn't seem to beat on its own and her hands had lost the steady grip needed to finish the job.

Could she be having a heart attack? Is that what was going on in her chest? Tight, hammering pain, shortness of breath, energy-sucking lethargy coursing through her body from her head down to her toes. And what was with that tickly tingling sensation at the back of her neck?

Maybe she was catching a bug.

She hoped she was catching a bug.

This man was dangerous, from the velvety timber of his voice to the muscular temptation of those naked legs.

Even his bare toes…what was wrong with her?

Bare toes?

Get a grip, girl!

Tempting, but dangerous.

Distance. That was what she needed between herself and this man, to get as far away from him as possible for her own peace of mind. She'd been happily avoiding any relationships for over ten years now. The hotel had been her safe haven and she would not let this - or any - man change that now.

One last twist of her pipe wrench was all she needed to finish the job. She gathered up her tools, scrambling to get everything put away in her suddenly-too-small toolbox, and snapped it shut as she sprang to her feet.

Sparing one glance toward the bedroom door, she rushed to get out of the room, closing and locking the door behind her as she made her escape.

He didn't regret his actions of last night in disposing of this particularly bothersome person. Mr. Corpse Number 7 had it coming. Somebody had to do something about it, the guy needed to go down. Some people deserved what they got.

Echoing through the early morning hillside, the

sounds of his shovel stabbing the earth, ripping the dirt from the surface and tossing it aside, gave him a powerful feeling. He was the only man on the planet. The only living one, anyway. The dead guy lying at his feet... well... he didn't really count anymore. The combination of cooler fall temperatures, moist ground and autumn leaves would help disguise his freshly created grave while Mother Nature digested the flesh and bones until it was nothing but a nourishing meal of compost in her belly.

With the hood of his dark sweatshirt cinched tight at his chin, his hair stuck to the back of his sweaty neck. He paused in his task, stretched his back then leaned on the handle of the shovel to check his handiwork, the shallow grave that would be the new home for the dead body of his latest worst enemy; the lump of flesh and bones which was once a living, breathing - but annoying - person. All he had to do now was heave the body in, cover it with dirt, sprinkle on some colorful leaves, and walk away.

Seemed easy enough.

The already tired muscles in his back screamed in protest as he hauled the body over his shoulder and hovered over the fresh dug hole, his latest masterpiece.

This was his moment.

His victory.

His chance to shine.

Each body he fed to the earth cleansed his soul of disappointment. The fragrance of death tingled at his nostrils; the early hints of decaying flesh, the metallic perfume of day old blood, and the delicious aroma of lightly singed skin after being touched by an old Bic lighter.

How quickly would human skin catch a flame and would it melt?

He now knew.

This discovery was a new treat he planned to try again soon!

Savoring the moment with eyes closed, a satisfying euphoria washed over him. This is what his life was meant to be; an empowering experience. Exhilarating. Dare he say...orgasmic?

The shattering sound of a snapping twig nearby yanked him from his moment.

He wasn't alone.

Panic made him drop the body in the hole and the thump when it hit the dirt rattled through his head as he turned to search the woods around him.

A woman stood with her camera pointed right at him, capturing him and his activities with the incriminating lens of her camera.

That was a problem.

Even if she hadn't seen him, her camera probably had. Though his face was partially covered by the hood of his jacket, he couldn't be sure.

This was definitely a problem.

As the woman continued capturing photos, he stood immobilized. He didn't want to draw her attention if she hadn't already seen him.

She turned, disappearing into the woods and he leapt into action, covering the body and leaving only a slight mound of dirt which he disguised with a cover of leaves. Then with shovel in hand he pursued the woman, unsure what he planned to do if he caught up to her, only that he needed to track her down

She was an unplanned complication in his otherwise well planned day.

He wasn't fond of complications.

He wasn't fond of things unplanned.

She was both and he was now forced to make a new plan to un-complicate things.

His frantic footsteps caught up to her as she wandered down the path, following the patterns of early morning sunlight as it filtered through the trees. Running to keep up, he almost stumbled over her as she knelt at the base of a tree, camera glued to her face, focusing on something on the ground.

Strangely enough, it seemed she still hadn't noticed him so he ducked behind a large tree. He needed to memorize her face for future reference. She was tall, maybe 5'9", and built like an athlete, her windbreaker jacket hanging loosely over her slim body. He guessed she was in her mid to late twenties, with smooth unblemished skin just slightly bronzed by time spent in the sun with a light dusting of freckles across the bridge of her nose. Light brown hair was pulled back in a high ponytail that swished from side to side as she walked.

She was so deep in concentration, he could have walked right up and eliminated her, his only witness, and been done with it.

But, no.

If he were to dispose of her here, it would probably bring cops swarming the whole area. Chances were this woman lived nearby and her disappearance would not go unnoticed.

The new addition to his collection had just been buried. The ground beetles hadn't gone to work at disposing of it yet.

Damn!

The cops would come in, discover the rest of his collection and ruin everything!

He needed a new plan.

She stood, packing her camera into the bag strapped at her shoulder, zipped up her jacket against the morning chill and walked away from him.

If he were lucky she would be done for the day and head home, giving him the chance he needed. He'd follow her home, find out where she lived, and plan his next steps from there.

It was easy to follow the woman down the path. They didn't venture far. An imposing structure rose up from a clearing in the wooded hillside, a very old looking hotel nestled neatly in the secluded area.

Thirty-one years living in the area and he'd never traveled in this direction before, never one to stray from his normal patterns. This was a new discovery for him. He knew his home, he knew the woods. A creature of habit rarely strays outside his comfort zone.

He held back, hidden by underbrush as he watched the woman until she was swallowed up by the front entrance of the massive structure.

The sign in front of the building pronounced it as The Manchester. Yes, of course. Anyone who lived around these parts for any length of time would have heard of the historic old hotel, even if they'd never seen it.

He studied the building, judging its size and how many people it could hold. The elaborate stone trim made it hard to read how many floors, but by counting layers of windows he guessed anywhere between three and five.

He would return home for now and come back in a couple of days and check into the hotel where he could keep an eye on the mysterious woman. He relished the idea of watching his prey from close by, possibly even befriending her before making his move.

Underbrush crackled under his feet as he retraced his steps back to his comfort zone, looking forward to the day real soon when he would return to this place and make himself at home.

The day when he would add another prize to the collection he'd buried in the woods.

****Chapter Two****

Danielle smothered a grin as she caught her first glimpse of the other woman. Though she'd grown accustomed to the daily Goth garb, each day was a new experience. Today Roxanna was decked out in a floor length sheath of slinky black material with long flowing sleeves and high collar wrapping around her head. It was apparently a day for embracing the fascinating concept of death again. Since the age of ten - when she had conjured her first ghost during an ill conceived séance in the back room of her family's funeral home - Roxanna lived her life in a delicate balancing act somewhere between life and the Great Beyond…preferring the Great Beyond.

"Seriously, Danni. The. Guy. Is. Hot."

"Okay, so he's good looking. Big deal." Danielle did not want to talk about Eli Garrison. Though she tried to portray herself as aloof, the snort she received from Roxanna told her she wasn't successful.

"Yeah. Whatever."

Danielle smiled at her long time friend and employee, enjoying their close relationship forged through rough times. Though they shared the common distinction of age and were unique in their ability to see the dearly departed who hadn't quite departed, they were physical opposites - Roxanna being petite pale skinned and dark haired, Danielle tall, tanned and brown haired.

"Sebastian welcomed him with his particular sense of charm."

"Oh no, not that!" Danielle imagined the horror of a new guest enduring the torture of Sebastian's gaseous personality. She could still remember the first time she'd encountered the twenty pound yellow striped cat. The only difference being that she could see the cat where their new guest could only smell him.

"Totally." Standing at the front desk, Roxanna's fingers were scratching through Sebastian's fur as they spoke, receiving a purr that rattled the countertop where he was always perched.

"Now, I've really got to get to work. That washing machine has been giving me fits. I need to take a look at it before calling a repairman and see if I can fix it first. Toss me the keys, would you?"

"No problem."

"Well, well, well. Now, what do we have here? Two lovely ladies looking for a good time?" Startled, both women swung around to face the figure belonging to a familiar masculine voice.

"Hey, Vic. Long time no see. What have you been up to?" Danielle asked the attractive man leaning on the counter adopting a flirtatious pose for the two women. Dressed in typical 1970's casual polyester from the open neckline of his loose shirt - which displayed his abundance of gold chains - to the tailored slacks, tight in the backside and well-filled-out in the front, his tanned hairy chest teased, hinting at a muscular torso framed there.

"You know…so many women, so little time. The Vic-man likes to keep busy." He puffed out his chest and ran a smoothing hand over his meticulously groomed hair.

"Cool down, Casanova," Danielle admonished. "You know we love you like a brother. Don't waste your pick up lines on us, we're not buying."

"Ah, what a shame, babe. A nasty shame…" and as quickly as he'd appeared he was gone.

"What a waste of delicious manhood," Roxanna com

mented.

"Yeah, he still knows how to work it, huh?"

"I'd do him." Roxanna closed out the cash drawer and carried the money to the office safe, tossing the ring of keys to Danielle as she left.

With the first step of his plan accomplished, he was now a guest at the Manchester complete with a fresh hair-cut, some clean clothes and a new name. The car he'd stolen was parked out front, the stolen license plates disguising it as efficiently as his new look disguised him. He hadn't seen his prey yet but he could almost smell her nearby, his senses on high alert. The girl who'd checked him in at the desk was a decidedly dark challenge with her black makeup and clothing, she looked like a sorceress and he got hot just looking at her. But no, he needed to concentrate on the other woman.

The hotel slumbered on, the only sounds from the second floor were his footsteps as he paced. He'd been in his room for a couple of hours and hadn't heard a sound from outside his room. Either the room was sound proof or the other guests just didn't venture out much.

That could work for him.

No witnesses. No interference. No distractions.

From one window of his room, looking out the back-side of the hotel, he could see across the Des Moines River. The hotel was ensconced on the hill overlooking it. Turning, he looked out the window at the other side of the building and he imagined seeing the mound of dirt he'd recently placed in the woods, though he knew that was impossible. He unlatched and pushed the window open, leaning out, and listened to the whispers coming from the woods, whispers telling him his secrets were hidden amongst the trees, beneath the under brush of fallen leaves. Secrets he'd buried in many trips to this hillside over the years, trips that had never revealed this hotel to him, housing this small community of people whom he had yet to meet but fully intended to.

He closed the window, sliding the lock securely in place, and stepped away from the view. He needed to unpack his meager belongings and get settled into his new temporary home, there was some exploring he'd need to do and nighttime was fast approaching.

****Chapter Three****

Like a tornado, she blew through her apartment, leaving each surface sparkling clean, ruthlessly wiping out any helpless dust bunnies before they had the chance to procreate and multiply.

It was cleaning day and Danielle attacked the weekly ritual with relish. Though maintaining every square inch of hotel property was a daily responsibility, the maintenance of her personal space was a special treat she reserved for every Friday. Rain or Shine.

Housecleaning was like a spiritually cleansing event. Twelve years of hard work around the hotel had given her the strength to put memories of abuse behind her. At least she thought the memories were gone, but every time she cleaned it was as though she were still scrubbing away at them, hoping to get rid of them for good.

The final step in the cleansing process was to take the bags of garbage out to the large dumpster tucked behind the hotel.

Grasping a bag in each hand, she bumped the door open with her backside and hauled them outside, shaking her head as she noticed the lid was off again, a sure invitation to the local wildlife looking for a free meal. She slung the bags in and slammed the lid shut before swinging around to head back inside.

In the next instant, the silence of the courtyard was shattered. As if in slow motion, Danielle felt herself lifted off her feet and thrown across the yard, her body slamming against the back wall of the hotel, ears and head pounding from the explosion.

Guests poured through the patio doors to investigate, but she was frozen in place, not quite understanding what was happening. Roxanna reached her first, dropping to her knees beside her.

"Danni, what happened?" Roxanna grasped one of Danielle's arms as she tried to stand, shaking off a round of dizziness.

"What? Oh, I don't know. I just brought out the garbage and walked away." Through her fog, she saw her guests gathering around them and a couple of the men stood by the twisted heap of metal where the dumpster used to be.

Her fuzzy eyes went to the taller of the two who had pulled out his cell phone and was making a call. Something about the man...the way he'd taken control of the situation... something in the way he was calming her guests and assessing the scene. It was reassuring but scared her at the same time.

The shorter man watched the other man then scanned the area, his eyes settling on Danielle as though he'd been looking for her.

Roxanna wrapped her arms around Danielle and helped her inside the hotel, sitting her in the nearest chair. "You wait right here, I'll get you something to drink."

As Danielle felt Roxanna slip away, another body approached, kneeling in front of her. Still trying to shake the throbbing in her ears, she lifted her eyes to face the man before her.

It was the tall man by the dumpster.

Dark tousled hair, chiseled jaw, five o'clock shadow and dark brown eyes. The tingling sensation in her chest told her this was boxer-shorts-man in room 2H, just as heart-stoppingly-gorgeous above the waist as she'd guessed he would be. His face was only inches from hers, studying her, hypnotizing her with his silence. Then he spoke, and his deep voice snapped her out of her shocked state as her body started trembling, her teeth chattering.

"Hey, my name is Eli. I just checked in here the other day. Are you okay? What's your name?" His gaze rolled over her then he called over his shoulder, "can somebody please get us a blanket?" Then he turned his attention back to Danielle. "Can you tell me your name? Where you are? What day it is? I've called the police - though I'm surprised this godforsaken place even has 9-1-1 service. They're on their way and paramedics if you need it." He seemed to be waiting for her to respond, so she nodded and told him her name. "Do you know what happened out there, Danielle?"

The nodding and shaking of her head was giving her the beginnings of a headache so she was grateful when Roxanna returned with a soda, aspirin and a blanket. Eli took them, wrapped the blanket roughly around Danielle's shoulders and handed her the aspirin and soda. Her body was already feeling the effects of her unplanned landing against the back of the hotel, she could feel the scratches and bruises she'd be dealing with later. Roxanna sat on the arm of her chair with one hand on Danielle's shoulder.

Eli silently studied Danielle then turned to face the circle of people behind him.

"Did anyone see anything? From what I can tell, we had an explosion in the trash bin. If anybody knows anything, now would be a good time to tell me."

"Who are you? Why don't we wait for the sheriff to come?" One woman asked.

"I'm Eli. I'm staying in room 2H upstairs. I'm a cop. I'll talk to the police but I'd like to get as much information as I can before they get here."

"Danielle's brother, Ben, is with the sheriff's department. He'll probably be the one to come. We'll talk to Ben when he gets here."

"Suit yourself. I'm going to go out and poke around. Keep an eye on Danielle, keep her wrapped up until the paramedics get here." He stalked outside not waiting for a response from the crowd.

Roxanna held herself stiffly at Danielle's side but remained silent with her thoughts.

"I don't even know what happened." Danielle turned to face the other woman. "What just happened?" When Roxanna remained silent, Danielle decided it was time to step up and make sure her guests were okay.

Standing, she rolled up the blanket and handed it to Roxanna. "I'm okay, I was just a little shook up there for a minute. It feels like my ears need to pop but I'll be fine, a little sore but fine. Could have been worse. Let's go outside and see what's going on. Oh wait, I need to call Ben."

"Already on his way."

"Oh, right." Tires crunching on the gravel driveway in front signaled an arrival. "I think they're here." Danielle rushed to the front of the hotel where she was engulfed in a bear hug by the big man who crashed through the front door.

"God, Danni! Are you okay? When I heard there was an explosion up here all kinds of images went through my head. Are you okay?" Sheriff Ben Jacobs set his younger sister away from him, frowning as he studied her face. Danielle could feel the cuts and bruises that were probably already forming on her neck, face, and bare arms and could only imagine what he was seeing. "The EMTs are right behind me. Let's get them to take a look at you before we talk."

At the mention of the EMTs, the front door swung open and they entered the hotel. Roxanna waved them over to Danielle then pulled Ben aside to talk.

"There's a guy out back. Says he's a cop. Just checked in the other day."

"Okay, that might be a stroke of luck. Maybe he saw or heard something that will help. You take care of Danni.

I'll go check things out in back. Thanks, Rox."

How did she know about the bomb and take it out-doors before it went off? He hid it in the perfect place, in a cabinet in the kitchen. It should have gone off in her apart-ment! That was the plan. If it had gone off in her apart-ment, maybe it would have destroyed whatever evidence she had against him, whatever she'd seen in the woods.

When he'd let himself into her place earlier that day he'd looked for her camera, film or a memory card but couldn't find anything. She must have taken it with her when she left in that rickety old truck she drove to town. If everything had worked out the way he'd planned, the bomb would have blown up most of her place and whatever wasn't damaged by the explosion would have been ruined by firemen.

What ended up happening was a pathetic explosion in an outdoor trash bin that only succeeded in making a mess and royally pissing him off. When he met that other guy standing by the scene, they discussed the situation inno-cently. Nobody would have guessed his part in the deal.

Then the cop showed up.

Another run of bad luck.

The woman had a brother who was a cop!

Could things get any worse? Maybe a good plan would be to stay close to the investigation. It couldn't hurt. He could even mention his own background in the National Guard.

Yeah, cops talked to other cops or soldiers, it just might work in his favor to bring up his military background.

He was just going to have to be more careful next time, and there would be a next time. He couldn't take the chance that she knew anything.

He had to clean up his loose ends.

The girl was a very loose end.

"Honey, you have to be careful. You almost got hurt real bad today." Ruth Manchester stood wringing her hands while her sister's head bobbed in agreement nearby. The Manchester sisters never appeared separately, their roly-poly bodies in flowered dresses were a matched pair of elderly spirits who had committed themselves to an eternity of watching over Danielle.

"And you two ladies worry far too much. It was just a prank by some kids. No big deal." As Danielle was relaxing in an overstuffed chair of the hotel, she tried to reassure the ghosts who had always been like family to her.

"I don't know…" Edna wasn't convinced but lowered herself onto the sofa nearby, joined by her sister, Ruth.

"Relax, Edna. Nobody was hurt. It just made a mess. Luckily the trash had been hauled away the day before or it would have really gotten messy."

The two chubby little ghosts disappeared and Danielle picked up the book she'd been reading, content to relax and enjoy the sounds of the night and the moans and groans of the old hotel with its collection of guests, both living and not-so-living.

"Hey, baby. What's a knockout like you doing in a place like this?" The soft, velvety voice spoke near her ear, tickling her neck with his icy breath.

"Vic. Hello to you, too. Original line by the way. Not. You need some new material." Danielle greeted him but didn't raise her eyes from the book she was reading. Agatha Christie. Her favorite.

It didn't take much to encourage the oversexed Casanova.

"Oh, baby…ouch! You wound this poor fragile heart. Be gentle with me, I'm a sensitive guy." She didn't have to look at him to know he'd place a hand over his chest and throw his head back for dramatic effect. The guy was all about drama. "When you gonna take pity on me and take me away from all this? Let me show you what romance is all about. I bet I could teach you a thing or two about love, baby. The Vic-man, he can show pleasure, he can take you to heaven and back, these hands can work magic."

"Beat it. I'm trying to read here."

"Okay, doll. But I'll be back."

"I wait with bated breath. Now beat it." Vic disappeared and Danielle smiled, enjoying their nightly ritual. Flirting with Vic had many advantages, most important of which was that he was safe and didn't expect anything she couldn't give him. His out dated flirting amused her.

The only other ghost keeping her company tonight was Sebastian, but as she searched him out on his normal spot on the front desk, he puffed out his chest, cast Danielle a haughty look, and disappeared.

The events of the day left her tired and ready for sleep, her bruised body reminding her tomorrow would be a painful one, but she wasn't ready for bed.

Something was keeping her awake, tense, and on edge.

She just didn't know if it was the bomb or the man in room 2H.

Eli Garrison hoped to take a walk outdoors before bed.

He hadn't adjusted to life outside the sweet musical sounds of the big city and was having problems falling to sleep.

He'd only made it halfway down the staircase when he heard voices...well, only one voice, but it seemed to be deep in conversation. Not wanting to intrude, he eased himself down to the carpeted stairs and waited, partially hidden by the railing. He recognized Danielle from this morning, the explosion out back. She appeared to be talking to herself, rather animated, while she was reading a book. Then she set the book down and stared off into space.

Something about this woman intrigued him.

As a cop, he sensed she had something to hide, her tough exterior set off alarms in his head.

As a man, it was something else that held him captive. She was stunning, a natural beauty, not like any of the women he dated back home in Chicago. This was a woman not concerned with her looks. Refreshing, almost innocent about it.

And now, here she was sitting alone in the lobby, late at night, talking to herself.

She rose from her chair and disappeared behind the staircase.

He still didn't know who the woman was – other than her name, Danielle   but now he knew she had her own apartment on the ground level of the hotel. Roxanna, the black haired, black nailed, black dressed girl was the only hotel employee he'd met. He suspected Danielle was more than just a guest at the hotel but further investigation was needed before he'd know her story.

****Chapter Four****

With wood polish and dust rag in hand, Danielle rolled up her sleeves and slipped from behind the front desk. Today was the day she'd be polishing the solid mahogany banister framing her favorite part of the hotel: the grand staircase.

Situated dramatically at the center of the lobby facing the front entrance of the hotel, the staircase rose from ground level, leading the eyes of the visitor upward to the second floor and beyond. Since everything above the third floor was closed off and draped in sheets to preserve everything from original furnishings to wallpapers and window coverings, she only concentrated her efforts on the first three floors. One of her few extravagances was the expensive oil she used to polish the original woodwork still remaining. She loved the sweet smell as she polished, the gleam of the rails and spindles, and the lingering feel of the oil on her hands when the polishing was done.

"So, Danni. We still haven't talked about the other day." Startled, Danielle dropped the wood polish when Roxanna spoke from the doorway of the office located behind the front desk.

"There's nothing to talk about." Bending down to get the polish, she hoped to avoid the subject by turning her back on the other woman, but it seemed Roxanna wasn't done with her yet.

"Avoiding the issue isn't going to make it go away. Somebody put a bomb in the dumpster. That's not something you can hide from."

"It's always been safe here, nothing like this has ever happened in the past, it's probably a one time thing." She kept repeating the words, hoping they'd be true.

Somewhere in the back of her mind she was beginning to worry.

His agent had suggested the accommodations, had even made the reservation for him. An open ended stay at an isolated hotel...in the wooded hills...on the banks of a river...in southeastern Iowa. It was about as isolated as a person could get. Nobody would find him here and he could get some work done on his latest book.

Eli quit the Chicago police force with the plan to devote himself fulltime to his writing but had succumbed to writer's block lately. His agent ordered him to stay at the hotel for as long as necessary to get the book done.

Something about this hotel was unsettling. Over ten years on the Chicago police force taught him to recognize details, especially when those details didn't add up. A bomb in the dumpster at a remote hotel in the woods did not look like a random prank by neighborhood kids.

There were no neighborhood kids.

There was no neighborhood.

The nearest town was at least a half hour away and Halloween pranks were usually carried out in the form of toilet paper or eggs, not bombs. He hadn't seen any kids since he'd passed through the town on his way to the hotel. There were only adults living in the hotel as far as he'd seen and none of them under the age of twenty-five. He didn't know how old that skinny kid was who did repairs around here but he doubted he was under twenty.

Another problem with the scenario was the collection of guests he'd met. They all seemed too flaky to have carried out a bombing or have the knowledge to build the bomb in the first place.

Either way, he planned to keep an eye on the place and its residents. He may have left the police force but he'd always be a cop.

Maybe a drive into town would get him some answers or some insight into the background of the long time guests at the hotel. If he was lucky, he might just get some material to get him started on his book.

It looked like it was time for him to take a drive into town.

He'd been a guest at the hotel for a little over a week now and was itching for his next opportunity. If his guess was right, she would wait for most of the guests to leave in the middle of the day and she would vacuum the carpets on the upper floors. The woman was a clean freak, there wasn't an inch of this hotel that wasn't spotless, polished, gleaming, or sterilized. That made it easy to figure out her schedule; everything she did was organized with almost military precision.

Deliciously predictable.

It would be perfect.

Neat and tidy.

He'd shove her down that insanely long staircase and she'd be dead before she even reached the bottom, before anyone would be the wiser. The hotel was typically de-serted during the daytime. He didn't know where all the other guests disappeared to during the day, he was just grateful they did.

With his hands steepled in front of his face, he pic-tured the scene from the privacy of his second floor room.

Wait a minute.

Somebody was out in the hallway, the jingling of keys as they opened the utility closet across from his room...it had to be her!

It was time to put his plan into action.

Cracking open the door of his room, he peeked outside to confirm his suspicions. Sure enough, she was hauling the industrial sized vacuum cleaner out of the closet and plug-ging it in.

He waited until she turned on the monstrous contrap-tion, the deafening roar drowning out any sounds except the beating of his anxious heart - or was that something only he could hear?

As she neared the top of the staircase, he inched out of his room. Pulling the door closed behind him, he made the short trip across the thick carpet, making sure to stay out of sight behind her.

Back and forth she pushed the roaring monster, leav-

ing triangular patterns in the carpet, sucking up anything in its path as she pushed it over the top of the stairs and pulled it back, pushing it to the edge, pulling it back again until she was standing at the wide opening at the top of the staircase.

She turned away from him and he made his move, lunging for her, intent only on delivering a strong shove that would send her head over heels plummeting down the mountain of stairs.

He'd played it over and over in his head.

He knew exactly how it would work.

That's not the way it happened.

As he lunged for her, she turned sharply in the other direction away from the staircase and he found himself flying through the air face first down the staircase, gravity mercilessly pulling him until his body finally made contact with carpeted mahogany halfway down the staircase. From there he rolled head over heels - just as he'd pictured her body would - until he landed in a painful, but very much living, heap at the bottom.

He lay for a moment, stunned.

Amazed that he'd survived, he dragged his battered body back to his feet and looked up the stairs where his intended victim resumed her chore, unaware of his unin-

tended downward flight.

Man!

He just couldn't catch a break!

He was a failure at being a soldier and now he couldn't even kill a silly little woman! It was embarrassing really.

He had several bodies buried in the woods nearby to attest to the fact that he was an able killer. What was it with this woman anyway?

As he stood gazing up the mountain of stairs, a sound from the front desk jerked him to attention. What he did not need right now was another witness! He spun around and lost his balance, dropping back to the floor.

Had he just heard a cat hissing at him?

No way!

Now he was hearing things?

Damn!

And what was that smell?

What was happening to him? Suddenly he can't kill one woman, then he's hearing things that aren't there and now he can't even control his body from stinking up the place with sneaky farts?

Shaking himself off, he put one foot in front of the other, dragging his body back up the staircase for an evening of recuperation and recon in his room. Every muscle, tendon, and joint in his body screamed in pain.

He was going to have to make another plan.

If he couldn't take care of her inside the hotel, maybe a change in location was needed. He'd get her outside the place.

Then he remembered hearing her say she was heading into town the next day.

That would be it!

The hilly roads into town were a perfect place to make somebody disappear and the added bonus was that everyone would assume it was an accident.

If they found the body.

He wiped the grin off his face as passed the woman on the way to his room, she nodded a greeting and turned away with a slight dance. The stupid broad actually seemed to enjoy vacuuming!

Yes, this new plan would work.

It had to work.

For now, he would check out his injuries and soak in a hot tub.

He was going to hurt tomorrow but it would be worth it.

"That was a close one, sister. He almost ran right into her; he could have knocked her down those stairs!" Edna commented from the top of the staircase as they watched the man let himself into his room and close the door behind him. "If you hadn't pushed him at the last minute like that he might have hurt our Danielle."

"Yes, Edna. You're absolutely right. What a clumsy man. One minute he's walking just fine then he suddenly takes a tumble almost knocking her down. Very clumsy of him." Ruth shook her head in dismay.

"It sure is a good thing we were here."

"Yes, dear. It sure was."

They checked on Danielle as she continued vacuuming then faded out as quickly as they'd appeared.

****Chapter Five****

The next day, Eli passed the rickety old truck on the way to his Mustang, recognizing the jean clad backside hanging out from under the hood of the truck as that of the kid who had worked on his plumbing.

So, at last count, the hotel employed Roxanna and a young repairman. Was that the extent of hotel staff? It was hard to imagine a place this size, and as well maintained as it was, not employing a small staff of workers. The landscaping alone would require a full-time gardener.

With a shrug, he folded his body behind the wheel of the cherished sports car he'd restored as a teenager, a cherry red 1965 Mustang convertible. He recalled the long hours of hard work to pay for the car, then two jobs once he'd graduated from high school before putting himself through police academy and following in his father's footsteps to become a cop.

Until recently, he thought he was happy. By day he got to catch the bad guys and save the world. By night, he made a respectable living writing about it.

Then he got tired of dealing with bad guys.

He'd become known as the reclusive author of crime fiction, Dirk Remington. Nobody really knew much about him and he preferred to keep it that way.

Last night he sat down at his laptop to write and found his creative muse was back. Staying up past midnight he finished several chapters before crawling into bed in the early morning hours. He woke late this morning and when he checked his kitchen for breakfast, found his supplies low. Skipping breakfast with the plan to head into town later for groceries, he sat down at his computer and kept writing, not stopping until the midday light creeping through the blinds reminded him he needed to get to town.

He started the car and sat for a minute, enjoying the purr of the finely tuned engine and the vibration of the powerful toy. With hands gripping the steering wheel he let the heartbeat of the classic muscle car hum its way up his arms and settle in his chest.

Yeah, he loved his car.

Putting it in gear, he backed out of his parking space

and turned onto the road that would take him to town.

"Thanks, Mrs. Meeker. And thanks for having Billie load my stuff in the truck for me. I'd better be heading back home before it gets too dark out there. I'll try to get back in town next week and pick out a turkey. Thanksgiving's not that far away and I want to fix a nice dinner this year for my guests." Danielle told the town storekeeper who'd known her since she'd first arrived at the hotel.

"You do that. Now run along. That hillside road just isn't safe after dark, I'll worry sick knowing I kept you here too late and caused you to have to make that drive in the dark. Be careful."

"Thanks."

Danielle bundled her small packages under her arm and left the store, letting the screen door slap shut. Her truck sat idling at the curb.

"Thanks, Billie. I appreciate it." She slipped the teenager a few dollars and climbed into her truck.

Pulling out of the parking place slowly, she watched her rearview mirror for traffic and eased on to the empty street. Her truck found its own way onto the familiar paved road and settled into the trip up the winding hill to the hotel while she unhooked her seat belt and reached for the radio to find a channel she liked, not bothering to refasten her seat belt.

Lulled by the peacefulness of the drive, she didn't hear the other car until it slammed into the side of her truck, nearly pushing her off the road in one swipe.

If she hadn't felt the impact of being hit, she wouldn't have known what had just happened. Without her seatbelt, she was thrown across the slippery vinyl bench seat, landing on the passenger side of the truck as the truck rolled to a crawl in loose gravel at the side of the road. Momentarily stunned but anxious to get the truck stopped before it took her down the steep ditch, she grabbed the back of the seat to pull herself across to the driver's side.

Before she could buckle herself in, she was slammed again, the truck shoved to the edge of the ditch.

Had the car turned around and come back for her? That would mean it wasn't an accident. Somebody had intentionally tried to run her off the road.

In her side view mirror she saw the blur of a car as it spun around with a screech of its tires, the driver burning rubber with smoke billowing out behind him.

He was coming back for her.

Pure adrenaline spurred her into action as she pulled back onto the pavement, her foot pressing the accelerator to the floor.

She was in a race for her life.

The sun reflecting off the truck's chrome hood trim made it difficult for her to see so she was driving on instinct while trying to make out the shape of the car she knew was pursuing her, the roar of its newer engine gaining on her in the old truck.

But she had an advantage over the other guy.

She knew these roads like the back of her hand and was counting on the dip in the pavement around the next curve. If the other guy hit it at the right angle and at the speeds they were traveling it would be hard for him to keep it on the road.

Her hands gripped the steering wheel and she leaned in, wishing she'd taken the time to refasten her seat belt, but not even trying to tackle it now.

That blemish in the pavement was just around the curve.

Just a few more feet and she'd be there.

The truck raced around the sharp curve and she yanked the wheel hard to the left, avoiding the hole and fighting to keep the truck on the road as she drove on.

Sneaking a peek in her mirror she saw the dark form of the car when it hit the hole, just as she had hoped, spinning out of control. She slowed her truck to a stop and turned in her seat to watch as the guy lost it, his car caught in the gravel at the side of the road then flipped over, tumbling over the edge and disappearing down the embankment with the sound of crushing underbrush. Then silence.

Her heart hammered in her neck and chest, an almost sickening beat, and she struggled to take a deep steadying breath. She'd call Ben when she got home and let his men check for survivors, right now she just needed to be far away from this place. Spitting gravel under spinning tires, she jammed the accelerator to the floor and didn't look back.

With brakes screeching to a stop in front of the hotel, Danielle wrestled the mangled door open with a groan of twisted metal and kicked it shut behind her.

Eli pulled his Mustang in behind her truck, skidding to a stop and killing the engine. Climbing from his car he stalked to her side, his eyes assessing the damage to her truck in passing before sweeping Danielle's shaking form.

"So, what the hell was that all about?" he growled, but Danielle didn't stick around to talk to him, rushing for the front door of the hotel. "Hey…" Forced to stand and watch her retreating form or follow, he reached the front door as it was shutting behind her.

"Hey, stop!" He fell back a step when she spun on him unexpectedly. "What was that crazy driving all about? You could have hurt somebody driving like a maniac!" Eli demanded, shoving his angry face in close to Danielle's.

"Jesus!" He caught her just as she collapsed to the floor, lifting her in his arms.

"Danni!" Roxanna gasped. Eli didn't see where she came from but was glad she'd appeared, pointing him toward Danielle's apartment.

"Here, follow me." Roxanna led Eli from the lobby and to the privacy of Danielle's apartment where he deposited the pale girl on the sofa.

"What did you call her?"

"What? Oh, Danni, it's short for Danielle," Roxanna said, but was focused on her friend who was starting to wake up.

"...Danni...sure, of course. So, does she, by any chance do plumbing repairs around here?"

"Of course she does. She owns the place."

"She owns the place?" That he hadn't expected. "Look, she's coming around." Eli stood behind the sofa watching as Roxanna sat cross-legged on the floor in front of the sofa holding Danielle's hand.

"Danni?" Roxanna whispered. "Are you okay?"

"…what?…Rox? Where am I? What happened?" Danielle asked and tried to sit up but Eli pushed her back down on the cushions.

"Whoa, relax there…take it easy." At his touch, she recoiled instantly, heated venom in her eyes, so he stepped back and let Roxanna take charge, confused at the animosity radiating from the girl.

"Danni, what happened?"

"Rox! You have to call Ben! Somebody just tried to run me off the road and he went down that ditch by the curve, you know where that hole is? Get Ben over there."

"I'll call Ben. You calm down. I'll get you some cocoa and you just sit there and drink it until Ben gets here."

Danielle glanced sideways at Eli, standing behind the sofa. He chose to stay quiet and stared back. "Rox, who is this guy and what is he doing in my apartment? You know we don't let guests in our apartments."

"Be nice, Danni." Roxanna handed her a mug of cocoa.

"I'm Eli Garrison. I'm staying in 2H, remember? I guess we haven't officially been introduced. We met that other day, out back when your dumpster blew up." He growled at her and at himself for just realizing that his ongoing damsel-in-distress was none other than the skinny repairman he'd only caught glimpses of up until now. As he recalled the two times he'd only seen her from the waist down and in baggy overalls, he was amazed that he hadn't recognized this incredible female form hidden there. His arms were still tingling from the contact of carrying her warm body. His heart still hadn't calmed its thundering beats and he was sure they could see that vein throbbing in his neck.

"So, do you have a death wish or have you just royally pissed off some ex-boyfriend who wants to see you dead?" His aggravation had taken the form of anger directed at this woman. This was supposed to be a quiet peaceful retreat where he could get some writing done. Instead, here he was for the second time this week getting involved in this woman's problems.

He faced her over the back of the sofa with arms crossed at his chest, biceps flexing in frustration against the tight fitting sleeves of his chambray shirt, and he could feel a muscle starting to twitch in his left eye.

"What? No. What are you talking about? Rox? Just who does this clown think he is, anyway?" Danielle pushed herself to her feet in an obvious attempt at intimidation.

He wasn't intimidated.

He glared back at her.

"Calm down, Danni. I've called Ben. Play nicely with Mr. Garrison until your brother gets here."

"Brother? Just who is her brother?" Eli asked.

"You met him the other day. Sheriff Ben Jacobs."

"Oh. Yeah. I'd like to talk to him. I was right behind her on the drive up here."

"Sure," Roxanna said. "Would you like a cup of hot chocolate? My friend, Danielle, seems to be suffering from bad manners today." She scowled at Danielle.

"Why thank you, Roxie. Yes, I would love a cup of hot chocolate." He ignored Danielle and followed Roxanna into the kitchen, leaving Danielle stewing on the sofa.

Danielle mulled over the events of the past few days. Could the accident have been more than an accident?

Of course.

The other driver was determined to run her off the road.

Was he trying to kill her?

No.

Well, maybe.

But was he targeting her specifically or was she just in the wrong place at the wrong time? Those were the questions she needed answers to and she didn't need the aggravating, sexy, bossy, hot, intrusive, hot, controlling, hot man in the next room to get in the way. The man with the big strong arms and sexy grumbly voice who'd carried her into her apartment when she'd fainted. Why did he have to be so...so...hot?

How embarrassing.

She'd never fainted in her life. Only weaklings and cheerleaders fainted.

She was neither.

She was a strong independent woman who didn't need a man in her life.

Except Ben.

Ben was the only good man in the world.

****Chapter Six****

"So, Sheriff. What do you think? Did you find anything at the crash sight?" Eli asked Ben as they stood in
front of the hotel.

"They found the car at the bottom. It was burnt to a
crisp so it will be hard to identify. If I had to guess, I'd say
the gas tank exploded when it hit the bottom. When daylight comes we can start scanning the area better."

Eli could only imagine the charred mess at the bottom
of the ravine, he doubted they'd get any evidence to help
with the investigation.

"So, you're a Chicago cop. How did you end up
here?"

"Quit the force recently, now I'm a writer. I came up
here to get a book done."

"A writer, huh? Eli Garrison. Hmmm... Garrison.

Would I know any of your work?" Eli admired the persistence of the sheriff in getting answers, but that didn't mean he'd give the man any more information than he had to.

"Maybe you'd know me best by the name of Dirk Remington."

"The crime writer, Dirk Remington?"

"Guilty. Listen, I'd appreciate it if you kept that to yourself. I really do need the peace and quiet, and my agent would appreciate that I make my deadline."

"Of course. No problem. As long as it doesn't get in the way of my investigation." Ben frowned and Eli guessed there wasn't much that got by this small town lawman. "You have quite a reputation."

"I'd like to think you mean that in a good way."

"We'll see." Ben leaned back on the hood of his car, crossing his arms at his chest before speaking again. "Look, something is going on up here. I don't know if my sister is the one being targeted but it's beginning to look like a distinct possibility. Until we get a handle on things, I'd feel better if I knew somebody was keeping an eye out for her when I can't be here."

"Well, from what I've gathered in the short time I've been around your sister, I'd say that wouldn't go over too good."

"Yeah," Ben winced. "You figured that out already, huh?"

"Been at the receiving end of it." Eli was actually beginning to enjoy his encounters with Ben's sister, but he wasn't stupid enough to admit it to the man in the sheriff's uniform who had biceps bigger than tree stumps.

"I just want you to keep an eye on her, keep her safe. If I hear you've touched her, I'll kick your ass and *then* throw you in jail."

"Right."

"I'll follow up with you tomorrow when I get some information on that wreck. Right?"

"Sounds like a plan."

"Oh, and you can call me Ben. We're not very formal around here."

"Sure, Ben. Don't worry. I'm not going anywhere."

Eli returned to the warmth of the hotel lobby after watching the sheriff climb into his car and drive away.

Danielle watched from the window as the two men shook hands, slapped each other on the back, and parted company just like old friends. She hated the good-old-boys club! They were up to something and it involved her. She didn't like it. Her overprotective brother was keeping information from her and getting chummy with that new guy. They forced her to sit on her couch while the big-strong-men brought things in from her truck for her, told her to "take it easy" and "let us take care of it." They were lucky they hadn't added "don't worry your pretty little head over it" or she truly would have decked somebody!

She knew she'd get nowhere forcing the issue.

When Eli entered the lobby, she turned away from the window and walked back to the front desk, ignoring him.

"Good night, Danielle," he called down as he climbed the stairs. A not-so-feminine snort was all he got in reply.

Okay, now he was really getting pissed!

She'd outsmarted him yet again!

It had been rough getting himself out of the ditch. He'd caught a break when the car blew up on its own after he'd been thrown from it on the roll down the ravine. That should slow the cops down but it was only a matter of time before they dug up some other clues. The car would have to be replaced. Maybe he could walk down the road a stretch and catch a cab.

What was he thinking?

There wouldn't be any such thing out this far!

He'd worry about that later. Right now he had to fo-

cus on getting himself back to the hotel and into his room before anyone was the wiser. If he remembered correctly, they locked the lobby doors around 10:00. His crushed watch didn't help him with the time thing and the full moon filtering through the wall of trees made it hard to judge what time he was dealing with, but he doubted that he'd been down in that ditch for more than a couple of hours. That would put the time a little after 9:00.

He kept walking, stumbling occasionally and sending a whole new level of pain through his body. The injuries from his tumble down the stairs were just kicking in and now he had a new batch of misery to deal with.

In his head, he could hear the whining voice of his mother telling him what a worthless failure he was, a pathetic loser who would never amount to anything. He'd tried to join the National Guard to prove her wrong. Just a few months into the training, the damn gun he'd been issued went off and shot him in the foot.

Okay, so maybe it wasn't just that one time. But the only person he'd ever hurt with his accidents was himself.

Things went downhill from there.

He'd been forced to move back in with his mother to recuperate. The Guard sent him a letter telling him - in so many words - not to bother coming back.

His mother read the letter to him as he lay in her spare bedroom, the whining sound of her voice grating on him.

Her condemning look and her sigh of contempt sealed her fate.

Hers was the first body he'd buried in the woods.

She now had plenty of company.

He'd lost count of those who had pissed him off.

The utility guy who came around to the house to read the meter. That guy was asking for it when he said he needed to check things in the basement. He couldn't let him into the basement. That jogger guy from the park was down there. There hadn't been time to dispose of that one yet, then he had two to deal with.

That neighbor guy who kept blowing around his leaves, early on a Saturday morning, with that obnoxious loud machine strapped to his back. Everybody said how annoying that was, he felt he'd done the neighborhood a favor in getting rid of that guy.

And then there were those two guys in the black pants, white shirts and black ties on the bicycles preaching at him when he opened his front door to them. He was particularly proud of that catch. He deserved a trophy. But they didn't even put up a fight. They spouted something about it being

God's will. Getting them to the woods posed a challenge, but borrowing his mother's station wagon did the trick. She really didn't need it anymore.

Now he was faced with a woman who just wouldn't die. He could barely even remember why he wanted her dead, he just knew she had to go.

One torturous step in front of the other, he trudged up the hill. When he was sure there were no cars coming, he walked on the side of the road where the ground was easier to walk. He would be able to dash into the cover of the woods in time if he heard a car coming.

Limping heavily on his bad foot, he just kept walking, hoping he'd be able to sleep in his rented room tonight and not in the woods somewhere, locked out of the hotel.

He quickened his pace just in case.

****Chapter Seven****

"I'm going to work in my apartment this morning, Rox. Will you be okay without me?" Danielle had just finished paying the bills and was looking forward to relaxing. All was quiet around the hotel and she grew restless. Most of the guests were resting in their rooms or had driven into town.

"No problem." Roxanna didn't bother to look up from the book she was reading as she stood behind the front desk. Sebastian's purr rumbled through the otherwise quiet lobby as Roxanna's fingers absentmindedly burrowed in the thick fur around his neck.

"I want to look at the pictures I took the other day. I haven't had a chance to even download them yet."

"Hmm."

"I'll just get these pictures printed and run them by

you and I'll be right back to work. Give me a couple of hours." Danielle knew she was stating the obvious, but when she couldn't get a reaction out of the other woman, no matter how hard she tried, she knew it was time to give up.

"Um, hmm."

A chill in the air announced they were no longer alone.

"Morning, Edna, Ruth." Danielle greeted the two ladies as they appeared nearby, finally grateful she had somebody to talk to who would actually talk back.

"Good morning," they said in unison. "We stayed up all night and patrolled the place for any suspicious activity. The place was quiet. We just wanted you to know that."

"Thanks, Ruth. It's good to know you're looking out for us, but really…I don't think we have anything to worry about here. These little accidents are just that - accidents." Danielle rushed to reassure them, but they disappeared as footsteps sounded on the staircase.

"Good morning, ladies. Any more accidents lately?" Eli asked a little too cheerfully, focusing on Danielle's reaction after nodding a greeting in Roxanna's direction.

"Good morning, Mr. Garrison," Danielle replied frostily. "I'm glad you seem to find my misfortunes so amusing. Were you always so sensitive to a victim's distress when you were in uniform?" she tossed back at him.

"My, my, my…somebody's prickly this morning." His amusement only irritated Danielle, which seemed to amuse him even more. "I thought I would drive down and take a look around the crash sight, see if the sheriff's office has come up with anything more on your accident. Would you care to join me?"

"No, thank you. I have some work to do around here. I think I'll leave the police work to the professionals. By the way, I thought you said you followed me up the hill. How did you not see anything last night?"

"I don't know. I must have come upon you after the guy disappeared down in the ditch. All I saw were your taillights as they hit warp-speed, even my Mustang couldn't catch you. You really need to be more careful, I'm surprised that old clunker of yours even makes it up that hill."

"Oh really? Tell that to the guy at the bottom of the ditch." She tossed her head and walked away from him to her apartment, letting herself in and slamming the door.

"You seem to rub her the wrong way, why do you think that is?" Roxanna smirked.

"Don't know. I'm just trying to keep the girl from getting killed. Can you think of any reason she would resent me for that?"

"Long story. I, for one, applaud your efforts." Roxanna cast a dark assessing glance up and down his body. "Let me guess, Ben asked you to play bodyguard."

"Am I that easy to read?"

"Ben is that predictable. Classic big brother stuff."

"In the short time I've been here, I'd say he has good cause for concern."

"We've never had any trouble up here. Neither did Edna or Ruth."

"Edna and Ruth?"

"The Manchester sisters. They left the place to Danni."

"Sounds like this place has an interesting history and I'd love to hear it."

"Seems like something you should ask Danni." At his raised eyebrow, she shrugged. "But she wouldn't tell you."

Nodding in agreement, he headed for his car, looking forward to getting involved in the investigation. It was the one thing he missed about being on the force, the adrenaline rush of gathering information, solving the puzzle and catching the bad guy. Unfortunately, all his hard work didn't guarantee that some greedy defense lawyer wasn't going to put the scumbag back out on the streets on some technicality.

In the books he wrote, they always caught the bad guy and the bad guy *stayed* caught.

Fiction rocked.

He loved fiction.

Danielle loaded the memory card from her digital camera into the drive of her computer and waited for the images to load. As she sat watching her monitor, she went over the events of the past few days in her head.

An explosion in the dumpster.

Could easily be explained as a prank by the neighborhood kids.

If she had a neighborhood.

Or kids.

Okay, that one would be hard to explain away as prank or accident. Could it be a buildup of methane gas? She'd heard of those things happening.

Or, maybe not.

Then the accident last night.

Definitely not an accident, but she still wasn't convinced she was a target of any kind. That one could be explained away as a drunk driver. But where would a drunk driver come from? There weren't any bars in the area, and she couldn't believe they would travel up her hill in that condition much less turn around twice to come after her. No, a drunk driver might hit her once but she doubted he would be so persistent and go at her three times.

A beep from her computer told her that the pictures were loaded, they appeared one at a time as thumbprints on her 17" flat screen monitor while she sat watching.

Crawling out of bed so early in the morning had definitely paid off, the sunrise she'd captured was well worth it. She scanned each picture looking for imperfections and quality issues she'd need to work on later. Minor balance and composition she could fix - crop a little here, crop a little there - if they didn't pass her strict standards they just got deleted.

Half way through the collection of pictures, she spied something unusual and clicked on the frame to see the full sized version of the shot. Still not clear, it looked like a man standing in the woods, framed by the rising sun at his back. She zoomed in for a clearer look. The form was fuzzy but she was almost sure it was a man. He appeared to be carrying something.

She closed the frame and clicked on the next thumbnail picture, zooming in on the shot.

Gasping, she realized what she was looking at.

The dark figure was turned away from the shot but she could see the fuzzy face of a person hanging upside down over the figure's back.

She closed the frame and looked over the gallery of thumbnails. There were several pictures of the scene; she had no idea at the time that she'd been capturing these images.

If the killer - and if he was burying bodies, he must be a killer - was aware that she'd shot these pictures, she could be in very real danger.

Somebody might even want her dead!

They might even have already made attempts on her life!

She needed to call Ben, but he was supposed to be at the crash scene today. Should she risk calling him?

When had she taken the photos? Checking the date stamp she always marked on her pictures, she thought back to that day. Her jumbled mind drew a blank. Roxie was real good at keeping a daily journal. She needed to check her notes.

She rushed to the front desk, searching for the book they kept under the counter. Roxanna came out of the office when she heard the noise Danielle was making.

"Danni? What's up?"

"Shhh….quiet…we have to stay quiet…." she whispered, her hands throwing papers and books around in her search.

"What's going on?" Roxie whispered, kneeling beside Danielle and grabbing her hands to still her movements.

"Rox! Where is your log book? Your journal? Where is it? I need to see the log for the past month and I can't find it!" She yanked her hands free and continued her foraging.

"I have it in the office. I was just updating it. Calm down, I'll go get it."

"NO! I'll get it. You have to meet me in my place. I have to show you something! Quick!" Danielle ran in the office, grabbed the book off the desk, dashed to her apartment with Roxanna close behind, and for the first time since living there, locked the door behind her.

"Okay, Danni. Talk." Sometimes, Roxanna's perpetually calm, monotone voice really pissed her off! Danielle grabbed her hand, dragging her to stand at the computer, facing the monitor. She brought up the picture file and opened one of the pictures, pointing to the dark figure outlined there.

"There! See it! What do you see?"

Roxanna leaned in.

"Here." Danielle zoomed in as far as it would let her. "Now do you see it?"

"Looks like somebody carrying something over his shoulder."

"I know!"

"You know? What? I'm not following ya."

"We have to see what happened on that day. Did any strange people hang around the hotel that day? Was the killer here?"

"Whoa…killer? What killer?"

"Roxie! Look! He's carrying a body over his shoulder!" Roxanna leaned toward the screen, squinting to get a closer look at the pictures.

"Maybe."

"Find it in the book for me, Rox! My hands are shaking too much! Find that day in the book."

Roxanna took the book from Danielle, checked the date she'd given her and turned to the matching page in her book.

"Well, we had two people check into the hotel around that date."

"Who? Who?"

"Eli. Eli checked into the hotel a couple of days before that. A guy named Wally Parker checked in a couple days after." Roxanna ran her finger over the page, double checking the names. "This doesn't mean anything. We aren't even sure what's in the pictures."

"I know, Roxie! I know!" Danielle paced as Roxie set the book down and went back to studying the digital pictures.

"The pictures aren't real clear. You can't really identify the person…if it really is a person."

"He doesn't know that! For all he knows I have a clear picture of him! Somebody is trying to kill me! That bomb! The car crash…they weren't accidents! Somebody was trying to kill me!"

"Calm down. We don't know that."

"That's not helping me here," Danielle shrieked, then put her finger to her lips. "Shh, we have to be quiet. We have to tell Ben but we have to be careful that nobody else hears us. Oh my gosh! He's all chummy with Eli! For all we know, Eli is a killer!"

"No."

"We can't take that chance! The killer could be staying here, or not. But we can't take any chances! It could be any one of them, for all we know!"

"I don't know. Mr. Parker? He's kind of geeky looking. I don't see him as a killer. I'd say Eli looked stronger, though. Strong enough to carry a dead body over his shoulder."

"Oh my gosh! Why are we renting rooms to complete strangers? They could be serial killers! Rapists! America's Most Wanted for gosh sakes!"

"If we stopped renting rooms we'd be out of business."

"Well, until we can get to Ben we have to act normal. Act like nothing has happened. Try to keep quiet about this. I need to hide this somewhere safe." Danielle saved the file on her desktop then pulled the memory card out of the drive. "Where would be the safest place to hide this?"

"The office safe?"

"Think!"

"Call Ben."

"First I'm going to make a couple of copies of this card, stash them someplace. Keep this one on me, then we can give a copy to Ben. And do not tell anybody else about this."

****Chapter Eight****

"So, what have we found?" Eli relaxed against his Mustang as Ben approached.

"Well, not a lot. They're pulling the car up now." Ben nodded at the grinding sound of the winch pulling the car from the ditch. "We'll impound it and go over it with a fine tooth comb, but I doubt we'll find anything. A couple of men are searching the area for anything that would help. Time will tell."

"Hey, Ben." One of his deputies shouted from the road. "I think you need to get up here and take a look at this."

"What have you got, Hal?" When they reached the deputy he pointed down at the pavement.

"Blood, by the looks of it." Ben and Eli knelt beside the brownish spots.

"Sure enough, hopefully human. Good work. Looks like we got the break we were looking for. The guy left us a trail of blood and my guess is that we're going to find it leads up this hill and right to the Manchester Hotel." Ben cursed under his breath. "This isn't random. He's got some grudge against somebody up there."

"You got any idea just who that might be?" Eli asked, not liking the options.

"My guess, Danielle," Ben said. "That would explain the bomb, and this accident. He was after her. She's the only one who'd be hauling garbage to the dumpster. And the car thing? She is the only one crazy enough to drive that rickety old truck, they had to know it would be her behind the wheel when they went after her."

"Yup. That's pretty much what I thought, too." Eli agreed as they faced uphill, their eyes drawn to the trail of blood leading in that direction. "We now have DNA and if he's in the system we'll find him."

"Spoken like a big city cop, but this is small town Iowa. DNA is not something we have the resources for. We have to send it in and wait."

"Where would you send it? Des Moines? Davenport?"

"Yeah."

"You have anyone in mind as a suspect?"

"Not you, if that's what you're asking."

"You had me checked out, didn't you?"

"The first day I met you I ran a check on you all the way back to high school. Do you think I would have left you with my sister if I hadn't checked? Chicago Police Department has nothing but good things to say about you. Just don't prove me, or them, wrong."

"You got it."

"Oh, and Eli?"

"Yeah?"

"Keep your hands off my sister."

Misery.

Unbelievable pain and misery.

He'd only been able to drag himself to his room after the hotel opened up the next morning. There had been too many people hanging around in the lobby so he wasn't able to sneak in undetected.

The night was spent sleeping in the woods. Watching the front desk through the front lobby windows, he waited until the coast was clear before he made his move this morning, dashing up the stairs as fast as his body would let him. More like an animal on all fours, but at least he made it.

Letting himself into his room, he'd locked the door with a scraped hand and it wasn't until he was facing himself in the bathroom mirror that he realized the full extent of bodily damage he'd sustained in the past two days. His clothes would have to be trashed, they were hanging in shreds from his bloodied body. Luckily, he didn't have any marks on his face that he couldn't cover creatively with turtlenecks or shirt collars. How he'd managed to get himself to his room without being seen was a stroke of good luck he hadn't encountered up to this point.

After soaking in a long hot bath, he reassessed the mess that was his body. There were scratches and bruises from his collarbone to the tops of his feet. Winter clothing would conceal most of it but at some point he was going to need to take care of that deep gouge on his leg, it probably needed stitches but he couldn't take the chance of asking for first aid or medical care. No...maybe he could run to town for bandages. Some butterfly bandages would be just as good as stitches.

But how was he going to get around when his car was a charred heap at the bottom of a ditch?

He would need to make an appearance of normalcy around the hotel, he couldn't afford for anyone to suspect something was wrong with him.

Damn that woman.

Why couldn't she just die?

Groaning as she disconnected the phone call to Ben, Danielle turned to Roxanna. They hovered in her living room, too paranoid to come out of her locked apartment.

"Eli is with him," she told Roxanna, hugging herself against the shivers. Roxanna sat relaxed and silent on the sofa, a steady Goth picture of inner calm.

"I still say it's not Eli."

"Yeah, but look at when everything started happening. The same time he appeared on the scene. You call that a coincidence? Too much of a coincidence."

"Let Ben handle it."

"Fine. I'm locking my apartment from now on."

"Whatever."

The sound of the doorknob rattling then her brother's voice, spurred Danielle into action.

"Danni? Your door is locked. What the hell?"

"Ben, thank goodness!" Danielle threw the door open but held herself rigid when she spied Eli over his shoulder. "Come in! Come in!" She dragged at Ben's arm, pulling him into the apartment and avoiding eye contact with the other man.

"Do you mind telling us what the hell is going on?" Ben's bemused look was echoed on the silent face of Eli, who stood behind him in the doorway. She rushed to shut and lock the door, pushing them into her apartment and out of the way.

"We have something you need to see and I'm not completely comfortable with Mr. Garrison being here, if you must know." Danielle glared at the big man behind her brother.

"I'll vouch for Eli." Danielle wasn't convinced, but had to bow to her brother's judgement…for now. "Now, out with it! What have you got?"

"Come here." Danielle motioned him to her computer, pushing him down in the chair facing the monitor screen where he could see the pictures already there waiting for him.

"Okay. What am I looking at here?"

"There." She poked her finger at the monitor. "I was taking these pictures in the woods the other morning and I caught somebody without realizing it. There, do you see him?"

As she pointed to the screen, Eli leaned over Ben's shoulder to get a good look.

"My God!" Ben exclaimed, then spun in the chair to

look at his sister. "You've had these pictures all this time?"

"I loaded them this morning from my camera. I was just taking pictures of the sunrise. I didn't even see that guy! Not until I looked at these pictures."

"Shit," Eli muttered under his breath. "You do realize that this is what we would call motive, right?"

"If by that you mean somebody is trying to kill me because of these? Yeah, Mr. Smart Man! I get it!"

"Ben. I'd say we have a little problem here," Eli said calmly, stepping away from the computer and leaning on the back of the sofa with his hands in his front jeans pockets.

"Ya think?" Danielle was just this side of hysterical. "I'm going crazy here and the man thinks we have a 'little' problem! Why is everybody so calm? Somebody is trying to kill me! How can everybody be so calm around here?"

"Calm down, Danni." Ben stood and reached for his sister, but she pulled away from him with an angry twist.

"Again...calm? Are you freaking kidding me? No, Ben! For all we know this guy here is involved!" Danielle poked an angry finger at Eli as she ranted out of control. "He appeared on the scene at the same time all of this started! How do we know he isn't some psychopathic killer?" She turned accusing eyes on Eli, who returned her look quietly but didn't show any emotion beyond the clenching of his jaw.

"Don't be ridiculous, Danielle! He's a cop, for heavens sake! The City of Chicago vouches for him. You're just upset, Eli is here to help." Ben faced his hysterical sister.

"Danielle." Eli interrupted. "Don't you think I've had plenty of opportunities to kill you if I wanted to? You leave your door unlocked for Christ's sake! You wander around the grounds alone. If I wanted you dead, you'd be dead," he informed her in his low gravely voice, taking his hands from his pockets and crossing his arms at his chest.

"Ben. I don't know." She dropped on the chair at her desk, her adrenaline rush draining all of the energy out of her.

"This is unproductive," Ben barked. "Do you have copies of these?"

"What? Oh, yeah. I made several copies. I just don't know what to do with them. Do you think we can identify him?"

"We need a copy so we can send it in with those blood samples to get analyzed. Do you remember where you took these shots?"

"Yes, I can show you. Wait…blood? What blood?"

"We found a trail of blood along the road, near the crash sight. We took some samples and are hoping to get some DNA. Meanwhile, we need to find this body he was burying, if that's really what's going on in the pictures." Ben started snapping and unsnapping the clip holding his gun in its holster. A sign, Danielle knew, that he wasn't as calm as he appeared.

"God! I didn't even think about the body. There's actually a dead body buried out there somewhere!" Danielle leaned forward, resting her face in her hands.

"Danni," Roxanna leaned down and whispered, close to Danielle's ear so she wouldn't be overheard by Ben or Eli. "We have company, other than the warm-blooded-and-living variety." Danielle lifted her face to look around the apartment, and spied Edna and Ruth hiding in the corner of the room. She shook her head at them, hoping they'd get the message to stay put.

"Uh, Roxie. Can you help Ben figure out where that location is in the picture. I need some time alone in my bedroom, to calm down. I'll be right back." Danielle slipped away from the room and motioned the two Manchester sisters to follow her into the bedroom, where she closed the door behind them for privacy.

"Ruth? Edna? Do you know anything? Have you seen

anything unusual going on around here lately?" Danielle asked. "Wait, what am I saying. Everything around here is unusual." They nodded in agreement but didn't answer her questions.

"So? What do you know?" Danielle repeated.

"Well, honey. This is all new to us, too. We haven't seen anything out of the ordinary. But then, we're bound to the inside of the hotel so we can only see what goes on…well…inside. If you have a spirit that can actually leave the hotel, you might ask them because it seems that everything that has been happening has all been outdoors."

"Yeah, yeah. You're right. But still…are either of you even catching a feeling of something? Anything?"

"No, honey. Sorry," Ruth answered.

"Okay." Danielle relented. "But from here on, keep an eye out for anything and everything unusual. I mean, other than the *usual* unusual, okay?"

"Of course, sweetie," Edna answered this time. "We feel terrible about this. Who would want to hurt another person like this? We heard you say there's a dead body buried out there in our woods! Disgraceful!"

"Danielle, sweetie," Ruth interrupted her sister. "You be careful, you hear me? And Roxanna, too."

"We will. Ben is on the case. He'll catch this guy," she

reassured the worried sisters. "Meanwhile, I'd better get back out there before somebody wonders what I'm doing in here." As she opened her door to rejoin the others, Ruth and Edna faded out.

"Here she is. Everything okay, Danielle?" Ben asked his sister without delving any deeper.

"Yeah, no problems. No additional clues either, sorry." Ben nodded, private message acknowledged. Across the room, she saw Eli raise a questioning eyebrow at the strange conversation but kept any questions he might have about it to himself.

"Okay, well then," Eli said.

"Eli, you want to walk me out? Roxie gave me a place to look in the woods, I'll grab some of my men from the crash scene and head on out there. No sense risking nightfall before we've had a chance to mark the crime scene…if we end up finding anything. A body, a grave or otherwise," Ben told Eli as they were walking from the apartment, leaving the two women alone to lock the door behind them as they left.

A commotion downstairs woke him from his painful sleep. He'd only drifted off briefly before he heard raised voices, then silence.

Damn.

He didn't know what was going on and that was a problem. If his plan was to work, he needed to stay on top of all activities around this place so there were no surprises.

Dragging himself upright in bed by grabbing the side of the bed, he pulled himself up and swung his feet over the edge. The screaming pain in every inch of his body forced him to sit for a few minutes before trying to rise to his feet. He wavered on his feet for a minute then shuffled to his closet to pull some clothes on over his nude body, making sure to cover as much of his bruised skin as possible. As he stood in front of the bathroom mirror, checking himself over, his fingers combed through unruly hair. He figured he was presentable enough as long as he didn't let anybody get too close, so he let himself out of his room.

Reaching the halfway mark down the staircase, he heard two male voices heading for the front door so he sat on the nearest step and peered through the banister. One he recognized as the guy who lived upstairs next to his room. The other guy was the local who had come out when the bomb exploded, the light from the old chandelier he stood under glinted off the badge pinned to the man's plain clothed shirt.

Evidently, local law didn't always wear uniforms.

He'd have to remember that.

It sounded like they were heading into the woods to look for something. Were they looking for his dead body? Did they think he had been mortally wounded from the crash and dragged himself into the woods to die? Or was it something else?

Damn! Damn! And double damn!

He was sure glad he'd moved that last body. It would really be a shame for them to find it and then start looking around and find the others. A damn shame. He moved it far enough away from the original spot that they shouldn't run across it. He hoped. The others should be good and decomposed by now, no more than bones.

He mentally crossed his fingers.

He couldn't afford for those cops to be snooping around in the woods! They would mess up everything! All his plans, they'd be ruined!

If there was to be a volunteer search party, he needed to get on it. Cops always arranged volunteers out in the boonies when there were crimes to solve or lost people to find, right? It wouldn't hurt to mention that he used to be in the Guard.

Maybe he could walk down the road and get himself

involved in the investigation. He could hitch a ride into town without raising any suspicions, that would be the perfect chance to get himself another set of wheels.

Energized, he picked himself up - glad that he'd thought to grab his wallet - and headed outdoors to take the long tortuous walk back down the hill. In sweat pants and hooded jacket he should be able to convince them he was just jogging. Sure, and he could explain away his limp as a jogging injury.

Excellent, he loved it when things just came together so easily.

As darkness settled on the hotel on the hill, the rays of the waning moon lit the front lobby. Several residents were enjoying their regular card game and engaging in friendly conversation. Behind the front desk, Roxanna was trying to fend off the eager attentions of Vic while Sebastian maintained his normal perch on the corner of the counter.

Danielle loved the evenings when they visited like this. Both the living and the not-so-alive-living. The hotel and its ghosts were her family and home. Roxanna was like a big sister to her. The calm, mature, stable influence to Danielle's quick temper and tightly strung personality.

Remembering back to the day Roxanna left the security of her family business - the local funeral home - Danielle still felt lucky to have her at the hotel. Roxanna's ability to see ghosts had crippled her professionally; she found it impossible to shut out the overwhelming presence of the many ghosts who passed through the doors of the funeral home.

"Danni?" Danielle shook her head to clear the memories and focus on the voice. "Your cell phone was ringing so I answered it. It's Ben."

"Yeah, thanks. I'll take it in the office." She jumped up from her chair and rushed into the office, closing the door for privacy.

"What did you find?" Eager to hear good news from her brother, she didn't bother with pleasantries.

"Hello to you, too, Danielle. We haven't found a thing yet. We're going to shut it down for the night and come back in the morning." Danielle could hear voices in the background, the sounds of rustling leaves told her he was probably still in the woods.

"Okay." It was hard to act anything but disappointed, but she appreciated the hard work Ben and his men were putting in. "We'll lock it up here soon. Listen, I don't want my guests to worry, can we keep this quiet for now?"

"Well, that shouldn't be a problem since we really

don't have anything right now to tell. But if we find something out here tomorrow, all bets are off. We have to inform the public if there's a killer out there."

"I know, I know," Danielle whispered into the phone, peeking through a crack in the office door to look at her guests, her family, her friends. "I don't want to put anyone in danger."

"And you won't. There's no evidence of a killer, no dead body. The bomb and your crash are nothing more than random at this point."

"Yeah. But, you be careful out there, okay?"

"Aren't I always? Listen, I need to go. Lock yourself in tonight and I'll check in with you tomorrow. And don't worry. I'm sure we won't find anything."

So engrossed in a losing game of solitaire at the front desk, Danielle was startled when Eli swung through the front door, bringing the autumn chill in with him. It was just before lunchtime and she had been waiting to hear some word about their search in the woods since Ben's phone call the night before.

"Morning, Danielle."

"Eli." She nodded stiffly. "So, what's the verdict from searching the woods? Have they found anything yet?"

"No. They plan to work until dark, but haven't found anything. Nothing to even suggest any activity at all out there." Eli raked his hand through his dark wind tossed hair. "I really thought we were going to find something."

Danielle studied his face, looking for anything that would ease her mind or clear him from guilt. Deep down she knew he wasn't the dark figure in the woods, but something still made her nervous whenever he came near. Something made her body tremble. Something caused an unexplained weakness at the back of her neck whenever his dark chocolate brown eyes met hers. Something left a trail of heat over her body when the autumn chill should be leaving her cold.

Her eyes wandered down the column of his throat, to the chest that teased her at the opening in his shirt with a dusting of dark hair. A strong neck pulled her eyes downward, wanting to see more, guessing at the muscles and strength hidden there.

Yeah, it was only because she was suspicious of him, that's all.

It couldn't be anything else.

As her eyes traveled back to his face it was to catch his gaze, an awareness there, and his eyes traveled over her as well. Hypnotized, she stood as his eyes covered the short distance from her face down her slim neck, to the opening at the V-neck blouse she wore, and stopped at her hands that lay on the countertop separating them. She felt the caress of his eyes on her skin, her face burned at the implied heat in his eyes when they returned to her face. He tilted his head to one side and a slow smile covered those delicious lips, obviously enjoying the effect he was having on her.

Damn him!

The smile snapped her back to attention and she steeled herself against his hypnotic stare, straightening her spine and throwing her head back to look down her nose at him, challenging him with her haughty glare.

His smile widened at the challenge.

"As I was saying, they'll work until dark before giving up the search." His voice had grown a little husky, and he paused to clear his throat before continuing. When she started to protest, he held up his hand. "I know what we saw, but there's not much else they can do if there's nothing to be found out there. Actually, you should be relieved they haven't found anything."

"But, they're still going to check out the evidence they've collected so far, right?"

"Yes, of course, but there's not much. And if they can get a clearer look at your pictures, we'll be able to wrap that up, too."

"I just want things to get back to normal around here."

"I don't see any reason why it can't, we don't have anything to suggest you're in any danger. Just use common sense about walking into the woods alone, driving that hill after dark. You know, until we know for sure."

"Fine." She turned her chin up stubbornly, not liking restrictions placed on her.

"That's not asking for much, Danielle. For your safety and the safety of your guests. Ben will stop in before heading back to town, just to update you after they shut it down tonight."

"Fine." She turned away from him, effectively closing him off.

"I have some work to catch up on in my room. If you need me, you know where to find me." He headed for the stairs, ignoring her muttered words of "like I would ever need you" as he left.

"He's only trying to help, you know." Vic spoke from where Eli had been standing.

"Oh, not you too! I don't need some big strong man to tell me what I can and cannot do in my own home!" Danielle hissed at the ghost.

"Hey, baby…I'm just saying. I'd be more than willing

to rescue a damsel in distress but, unfortunately, I seem to be locationally-challenged. Can't do much for you from inside this place if all the action is happening outside."

"But you just don't get it! I don't need to be rescued! I've been taking care of myself for most of my life. And I don't plan to change that any time soon! Got it?"

"I'm a lover not a fighter, babe. Now come and give good old Vic a kiss. Lay one on me, and don't be stingy with the tongue…"

"You're impossible."

"No, not impossible. I keep telling you. I'm very possible"

****Chapter Nine****

"Rox, I'm going to work in the rose gardens. The weather's perfect for it and I've been itching to get outside," Danielle announced as she passed through the lobby and out to the tool shed.

She paused just outside the front door to take in a deep breath of crisp autumn air. The air was so fresh, the sound when walking through the fallen leaves made her feel alive, and the threat of Mother Nature dropping her winter load of heavy snow marked the beginning of the holiday season.

Encased in ankle high work boots, her feet crunched through the piles of leaves as she made her way to the tool shed, pulling on her leather gardening gloves in anticipation. Unlocking and slipping the padlock and key into the pocket of her bib overalls, she ducked her head as she went inside. Everything in the shed was neatly organized. It was one of the first projects she'd tackled when the Manchester sisters had hired her as gardener and all around repair person, she couldn't function in a disorganized environment. The tools were always clean and maintained and the floors neatly swept.

Tossing the rake and other assorted tools into the wheelbarrow, she balanced the one-wheeled wagon out toward the first of the rose gardens around the wall of the hotel. Working in the rose gardens always brought back memories of the day she had shown up at the hotel looking for a job, having just run away from home at the age of sixteen. The Manchester sisters were crawling around on their hands and knees, meticulously wrapping and covering each rose bush in preparation for the harsh winter. Their faces, hands, and clothing were covered in dirt but they charmed their way instantly into Danielle's damaged heart. She stood before them, duffel bag thrown over one skinny shoulder and attitude to spare. They threw caution to the wind and asked her to work for them with room and board included.

Attacking the ground with her rake, she enjoyed the physical work involved in mulching the gardens with the leaves raked from the walkways and driveway. Come spring, they would wake from hibernation healthier than ever. As she scratched the ground free of leaves, she blocked out the sounds around her, concentrating only on getting the job done.

Eli debated whether he wanted to interrupt her work with conversation then chose to stand back and enjoy the sounds of her rake mixing with the sounds of the trees blowing in the woods, now free of their leaves. Considering himself a smart man, he knew Danielle well enough to predict that an offer of help from him would not be appreciated. The stiff stubborn set of her back as she worked spoke volumes. He'd likely get smacked upside the head if he offered to help, so he kept out of range of her rake and other tools.

As he contemplated this, a sharp popping sound caught his attention. Danielle stopped raking and turned toward the sound, only then acknowledging his presence with a scowl.

Eli knew that sound, only hesitating for a second before leaping into action, diving toward Danielle and wrestling her to the ground in the pile of leaves, covering her with his own body behind the cover of bare rose bushes.

"Get off me!" She pushed at him, swinging her fists at his chest.

"Be still, you little fool! You're being shot at!" She went still beneath him. "Keep your head down, will you!" Eli held her down with his lower body, propping himself on his elbows to try and find the shooter. Another shot pinged on the hotel wall a couple of feet from where they were hiding. He reached into his pocket for his cell phone, hitting Ben on his speed dial but maintaining his hold on Danielle.

"Ben? Eli. We're being shot at up here. What? No, I can't see anything. It seems to be coming from the woods, nothing long range. Danielle, right here, safe. You need to get up here." As he spoke another shot rang out, spraying them with dirt as it hit the ground inches from them.

"Danielle. We need to move. If we can get up against the hotel, maybe we can work our way out of range. I'm guessing he can't see us and is just shooting blind. Come on." He slid off her body to push her toward the wall of the hotel, keeping himself between her and the shooter until they were up against the front of the building. He rolled to face away from her with one hand on her hip to hold her in place while he scoped out the woods, looking for the shooter.

Damn!

Where was his gun when he needed it! Safely tucked

away in his room. He never imagined he'd need it when he took this unplanned trip outside just to stretch his legs.

Who was shooting at them?

Was it Danielle's bomber?

The guy who tried to run her off the road?

Were they the same person?

After what seemed like hours, sirens announced the arrival of a car screeching to a halt on the front turnaround driveway. Eli held her in place as he waited, listening to the sounds of footsteps crunching on gravel and leaves, running away from them into the woods.

Turning to face her, he smoothed the hair away from her face where it had come loose from her ponytail.

"Are you okay?" He scanned her pale face. At her quiet nod he held himself still over her, studying, watching, debating.

He should get up.

He should help chase down the shooter.

He should help Danielle get inside to safety.

He should check to see if everyone inside the hotel was safe.

He should have done any of those things, should have done *all* of those things.

Instead, he slowly lowered his head, capturing the sigh

that escaped her lips as he found her trembling mouth, while his body lay protecting her, supported on his elbows at either side of her head.

For the briefest of moments, he could have sworn she kissed him back. Her sigh fluttered over his lips as he closed his eyes, ready to feast.

Then she surprised him.

With the strength he would have never guessed this woman could possess, she slugged him!

The slim, smart mouthed, aggravating woman balled up her fist and landed a punch right in his face. His cop instincts had failed him miserably, and now he was sitting in the dirt, nursing what was sure to be a shiner later.

Danielle was standing over him, brushing herself off – as though wiping any memory of him from her body – and already turning to walk away.

"…Danielle?" a voice was calling her from somewhere near the edge of the woods.

"Over here," she called to the deputy as Eli pulled himself to his feet.

"Oh, there you are. Are you two okay? I got the call there were shots fired. Did you get a look at the guy?"

"No, we didn't see anything but you should have plenty of bullets to check out. He scattered them all over the place." Eli indicated the bullet holes in the wall and the ground around them. "How did you get here so fast and where's Ben?" From the corner of his eye, he was aware of Danielle putting some space between them, and couldn't help feeling angry. He'd just put himself between her and the shooter, and she couldn't stand for him to touch her?

"He's on his way, I was already heading here when the call came in. Oh, that should be him now," the deputy said as Ben's car pulled in next to the other car and slammed to a halt. "I must have chased the guy off. I checked at the edge of the woods, found a bunch of shell casings scattered around there and footprints. I think we can assume that's where he was standing but he made a hasty retreat when I got here."

Ben joined them just as his Deputy finished talking. "Are you two okay?"

DAMN IT!

The bitch just wouldn't die! And now she had that other guy always coming to her rescue!

Who the hell was that guy anyway?

Okay, he knew the sheriff was related to her. Damn inconvenient. He kept popping up at the most aggravating times and messing with his plans, then that other guy seemed way too involved with the broad!

He'd joined the hunt in the woods the other day, enjoying the irony of looking for himself in the woods. Pretending to jog down the hillside road, he "accidentally" happened onto their investigation then volunteered to help search for clues. It was truly inspired. Those dumb hicks didn't have a clue that the guy they were looking for was actually helping them in the search.

They'd believed him when he said he'd hurt himself jogging and even given him a ride into town where he was able to rent a car. A plain-Jane-neutral-colored sedan, just like the other one he had when he checked into the hotel.

He was so proud of his diabolical plan to park his new rental car far enough off the road that it would be undetectable to passing vehicles. It turned out to be a stroke of genius since those cop cars would have driven right by it. On foot, it was only minutes from where he fired his last shot at that irritating woman. Now all he had to do was stash the gun with the spare tire in the trunk and drive on up to the hotel as though he'd just returned from a trip into town.

Pure genius.

Nobody would question him, after all he'd volunteered his help in searching the woods so he had already ingra-

tiated himself with the locals. What his next plan of action in ridding himself of that woman was...well...that was beyond him at the moment. He should have been checking out of the hotel by now and heading back to his mother's house...his house. Someone would be missing him by now and growing suspicious, maybe even worrying about him in the neighborhood.

Or not.

He'd really never gone out of his way to make friends with any of the neighbors since his mother's death...uh, disappearance. When he'd finally been able to declare her dead and collect on her life insurance, his new unexpected wealth made it unnecessary. He hired all the work done around the house and yard so he didn't have any neighborly chats over the fence, and his groceries were delivered to his house so he found no need to meet people in that other public arena.

Things were looking good.

Until the neighbor woman's son came over, bragging about his acceptance into the Marines.

That was the final straw.

That was his dream and some snot nosed kid from right in his neighborhood was going to go off and live his dream where he had been thrown out. So what if he'd shot himself in the foot! Lots of people have accidents with guns. That didn't mean he was a danger to himself and others.

He'd promised to be more careful, but what had that gotten him? It got him a discharge letter and a "good luck in whatever path you choose to take" speech from his instructor.

Now here he was.

Damn woman.

He would not fail at this!

That woman would be buried in the woods if it was the last thing he did!

He would not fail at this!

He reached his car and climbed behind the wheel.

Wait a minute.

He had to stash the gun. He popped the trunk open and climbed back out. As he unscrewed the wheel cover to pull the cover up, it slipped out of his hand and crashed back down, the echo sounding well into the woods and rolling over the quiet hillside.

Startled, the gun fell out of his hand and under the car. As he dropped to his knees to go after it, footsteps crunching on gravel crept up on him from behind.

"Hey, Buddy. Need any help?"

He jumped, cracking his head on the back bumper and

rolling over on his back behind the car while his eyes traveled up the legs of the man standing over him to the badge pinned on the deputy's chest.

Bad luck had cursed him again!

"Uh, no, Officer. Thanks." He scrambled to get to his feet, kicking the gun under the car out of sight. "Just, uh, fixing a flat tire...all done...don't need any help. Thanks."

"No problem. Say, you're going to have quite a nasty bump there on your head. That was quite a crack you took on the bumper. You sure you don't need any help?" The deputy looked him up and down, glancing in the open trunk at the spare tire still resting there.

"No...fine...I'm fine. All done. I'll be on my way now..." he answered, hoping the deputy would give up and just go away. "I'm staying at the hotel not far from here. I'll be fine, really."

"All right then. You have a nice day, sir. And take it easy. These roads can be tricky if you're not familiar with them."

"Sure. Right. Of course. Thanks." He watched the deputy turn and walk back to his car where it was parked across the turnoff, waiting for him to leave before making a move. With a wave and one last glance in his rearview mirror, the deputy pulled away.

As soon as the cop was out of sight, he dove under his car to grab the gun just in case some other nosy hillbilly came wandering by. He stashed it under the spare tire and bolted everything back down in place, slamming the trunk shut when he was done.

Whistling, he walked back around the car to slide behind the wheel. Yup, he was so clever and those damned small town cops were so clueless. That cop had no idea what he was up to.

Why...a guy could get away with murder around here.

****Chapter Ten****

"Okay, so that was definitely not an accident. Somebody was taking shots at you. Not me. Not anybody else.
You. Do you have any idea why?" Eli stood over Danielle
as she sat on the front steps of the hotel, her knees pulled
tight to her chest with hands that shook. One of those hands
had just delivered the future bruise now throbbing on his
face. He almost wished she'd look up at him, see what
she'd done, but her eyes refused to meet his.

"If you'd asked me that yesterday I would have said it
has to do with those pictures, but now I don't know. I'm
just not a threat to anybody." Danielle eyed the crime scene
tape Ben's men had wrapped around the area. Eli knew
what she was thinking; this was going to be hard to hide
from her guests. "Do we need to put that tape up? I don't
want to alarm my guests."

"They were going to find out about things eventually." Eli felt her tense every time he spoke. "Just how much do you know about the people living here?"

"It was not anybody from the hotel. No."

"How much do you know about any of them? Anybody stand out?"

"Other than you and the other guy who checked in around the same time you did, I'd trust them with my life."

"Somebody else checked in recently?"

"Yeah, Wally Parker…quiet, average looking man. Keeps to himself. And you. Pain-in-the-ass, irritating, nosy, bossy…"

"We'll need to check him out." Her personal insults, though amusing, weren't going to help so he chose to ignore them…for now. "Here comes Ben, let's see what he has to say." Eli turned to face Ben as he approached, a frown on his face and his gloved hand full of spent bullets.

"Well, it looks like a 9 millimeter, must have used some kind of silencer. That's something that's not easily purchased on the street. You say you didn't hear anything until the bullets pinged on the wall and the ground around you?"

"Yup." Eli answered. "I'd say he definitely used something to silence the shots, but why?"

"Maybe he's a lousy shot or just wanted to scare you. Who knows? Say, that's a nasty bruise you've got on your face, Eli. You okay?"

"I've had worse." Eli rushed to change the subject. "A lousy shot, for sure. He wasn't that far away, even if he sprayed us with shots he shouldn't have missed us but he did. He's either a lousy shooter, or lost his nerve once he started shooting."

"Still...look at all these shots."

As they were examining the scene, a car pulled in.

"That would be Wally Parker. Has a room upstairs, checked in about the same time you did. He was out with the crew yesterday, volunteered to help search the woods, was a great help." Ben nodded at the man as he limped toward them.

"Hello, Sheriff. How's your investigation coming along?" Wally asked.

"Just fine, Mr. Parker. We're following up on some leads. Had another little incident here today. No offense, but can you tell me where you were, say, up until an hour ago? Just part of the investigation, I have to ask everybody."

"No problem, and call me Wally, please. I was in town checking out the sights, picking up a little local color. You know, tourist things. Had a little car trouble on the way up or I would have been here sooner."

"Of course, can anyone vouch for you?"

"Sure anyone in town, just ask. I ate breakfast at a diner, did some shopping at the general store, then walked around in the town park."

"Ok, thanks. Like I said, just standard questions. I have to ask everyone."

"Of course." Wally nodded again and limped into the hotel.

"You don't really suspect that guy, do you?" Eli judged the strength of the man. "He doesn't seem like much of a threat to me. I get the feeling he's not very bright and I doubt he's strong enough to carry a body into the woods."

"First of all, we haven't determined there was a body in the woods and second...I'm not ruling anybody out at this point. I checked you out but who knows? The only thing keeping you off my suspect list is the fact you may have just saved my sister's life. By the way, do you carry a gun?"

"It's legal, and yes, it's a 9 millimeter. You can check it out if you want to, it hasn't been fired."

"I wouldn't be doing my job if I didn't follow up on

it."

"Ben?" Danielle snapped. "Are we through with the mutual appreciation society here? Seriously, you two guys are a little too chummy, it's nauseating! Can we get back to why somebody is trying to kill me?"

"Ok, here's what's going to happen, Danielle, and you're not going to like it. When I'm not around, Eli is going to be your shadow. You don't go anywhere, you don't do anything without Eli. Consider him your personal bodyguard until we catch whoever is gunning for you." Eli watched as the storm clouds started forming on Danielle's face. The fight was on.

"That's not going to happen! And you know it! I can take care of myself. I don't need this overgrown gorilla following me around, crowding me, getting in my way."

"…and another thing…" Ben kept talking as though she hadn't said anything, putting a stop to her protests. "I'm bringing Tiny up here to live with you until I'm satisfied things are safe." Danielle hesitated in her protests and her face lit up.

"Tiny? Really? You'd do that?"

"Tiny? Who, or what, is Tiny?" Eli tried to interject but was ignored.

"Thank you, Ben! I'd love it!" Danielle threw herself

against Ben and hugged him.

"...uh, may I ask...who - or what - is Tiny?" Eli asked.

"I'll accept Tiny, but no way will I let this guy," she mentally aimed daggers at Eli, "get anywhere near me."

"Nope. That's not the deal. You get Tiny only with Eli. It's a package deal." Ben refused to budge.

"Uh, excuse me!" Eli barked, refusing to be ignored this time. "Does Eli get any say in any of this? And who the hell is Tiny?"

Danielle and Ben finally turned to look at him, grins on their faces.

He was starting to get a bad feeling about this.

"Why, Tiny is my puppy. You'll love Tiny. Everybody who meets Tiny, loves Tiny."

"Why do I get the feeling that the best thing for me to do would be to pack my bags right now, drive away from this place, and forget I was ever here?"

He had a *real* bad feeling about this "Tiny" thing.

"Well, he's smarter than he looks. I'll give him that," Danielle smirked.

"Play nice, Danni, he's going to be your constant companion from here on," Ben scolded then hugged and released her as he turned to leave. "Now I'm trusting you two to behave until I can get back later with Tiny and some supplies. And Danni, no more yardwork until I'm sure it's safe out there. I think I'd prefer that you didn't even leave the hotel unless absolutely necessary. I can get whatever you need from town."

"Fine. But Thanksgiving is coming and I already have everything on order in town, I just need to pick it up."

"I can do that. You. Stay. Put." Ben ordered his sister before turning to leave.

"Okay, you said you were bringing a puppy. What the hell is that thing?" Eli watched as Ben was dragged into the hotel at the end of a leash by something only mildly resembling a dog.

"This is Tiny. He's a Bull Mastiff. Don't let his size fool you, he's not even a year old, he's still got some growing to do." Ben boasted as though the dog was his child. "He's just a baby but has been through his obedience training so he'll be just what Danielle needs right now." Ben knelt beside the dog, who had dropped to a sitting position beside his owner. Giving the dog a rough scratch behind his ears, he stood as the dog quivered in anticipation.

"Tiny!" Danielle shrieked. Ignoring the two men nearby, she dropped to her hands and knees and wrapped the dog in a hug, barely able to wrap her arms all the way around the massive bulk of Tiny's neck and shoulders. "How's my baby boy? Huh? How's he doing?" The doggie rear-end wiggled as Danielle baby-talked to him, the two obviously happy to see each other.

"So, Eli. You want to help me haul some things in from the car while she watches Tiny?" Ben asked with a twitch of his neck, sending the message that Eli shouldn't refuse.

"Sure, right behind you."

The two walked out but didn't start talking until they'd cleared the front door, where they wouldn't be over-heard.

"Okay, what's the latest you've found out? I'm guessing you didn't drag me out here to help drag in dog food." Eli followed Ben to his car, watching the trunk pop open as they approached. What he found inside were several large bags of dog food.

"Well, actually, you guessed wrong. Do you have any idea how much food a dog that size consumes in a day? This trunk full of food won't go as far as you think. Come on, let's get these inside while we still have daylight." Ben started heaving one of the many fifty-pound bags of dog food over his shoulder and trudging inside with Eli close behind him.

"Okay, sis, where do you want his stash? Someplace where he can't find it because I gotta warn you, he will help himself if he's given the chance."

"Oh, in the office. Just pick a place and start stacking it. We can keep the door closed so he can't get at it." Danielle answered from where she was covered by over 90 pounds of slobbering, wagging, whining puppy. She rolled him expertly and sat up with him in her lap so she could watch Ben and Eli pass on their way to the office.

Too late, Danielle realized her bad move.

Tiny started barking and jumped away from Danielle, leaping toward the counter where Roxanna was absent-mindedly petting Sebastian. Sebastian hunched his back, hissed at the crazed dog, passed gas and disappeared.

"What the...?" Ben and Eli came rushing out of the office at the commotion, only to be greeted by ripe gas, calm puppy and two quiet women. "Holy crap! What died in here?" Ben waved his hands at the air in front of him while Eli pulled the collar of his shirt up over his nose and mouth.

"..uh, it must be Tiny. What have you been feeding this dog anyway?" Danielle said. Roxanna held her nose and backed away from the area with watery eyes.

"Geez, Tiny! Somebody light a match will ya?" Ben backed away from the area toward the front door and escape. Roxanna pulled a candle from under the counter and lit it, pushing it toward the end of the counter.

"Hey, wait up." Eli rushed to follow Ben outside.

"Whew! That was a close one. Come on Tiny. Let's go show you where you'll be staying for a while." With a gentle tug on his collar, the obedient puppy trotted along beside Danielle to her apartment, eager to please.

"So, what do you need me for? Nobody is going to mess with her now that she's got that beast as her constant companion." Eli asked Ben as he was getting ready to leave for the evening.

"A little afraid of the dog, Eli?"

"No, are you crazy? I think I'm a little more afraid of the girl than I am of the dog." Eli was quick to deny. His fingers twitched at his side, fighting to keep them from going to the bruise on his face.

"I need you to look out for her. The dog is backup. You can't be with her every minute, she won't allow that. But she will let Tiny be there. I know I'm asking for a lot here. I'm counting on your instincts as a cop."

"You got it. My agent's not going to like it but maybe I'll get some good material for my book out of this."

"Good. By the way, the investigation has kind of stalled until we get test results back from the lab. I'll let you know when I hear anything."

"Right."

"Okay. Well, I've got to head on back. My house is going to be real quiet without Tiny. I hope we get this case over with soon so my boy can come home."

"Yeah." Eli agreed but for his own reasons.

He wanted to see Danielle out of danger again so he could pursue whatever it was he'd only had a taste of behind the rose bushes.

The next day, Danielle was polishing the banisters and paused to pet Tiny who had claimed a spot at the bottom of the staircase to nap. He rolled over, silently commanding her to scratch his belly. His back foot scratched at the air with Danielle's strokes and he groaned in doggy ecstasy, bringing a smile to Danielle's face and Roxanna's where she looked on from behind the counter.

"What a big teddy bear," she baby-talked to the drooling dog. "What a big spoiled rotten teddy bear."

"He is such a guy," Roxanna commented. "Just

scratch his itch and he's yours."

"Yeah, he loves human contact. I'll bet it's driving Ben crazy missing him around the house."

"Mmm, hmm. Too bad he and Sebastian don't get along."

"Too funny. Sorry, Tiny. We had to blame that on you, but we couldn't very well tell them it was Sebastian-the-invisible-cat." The happy dog sat up, facing her with wagging tail and hanging on her every word. "Come on, boy. I think it's time for you to eat. You must be starving, you've only consumed three times your weight today so far!"

Tiny followed Danielle around the front desk to her apartment. As they neared her door, he started growling, scratching at the door of her apartment. Roxanna joined Danielle, standing back from where Tiny was attacking the door, his deep barks echoed the pounding of her nervous stomach.

"What the hell?" They didn't hear Eli approach until he was right behind them. "What's the matter with him?"

"I don't know, I was about to go in and feed him and he went crazy when we got this far." Danielle wanted to pull Tiny back and calm him down, but fear held her immobile.

"Hold on, step back. Let me check it out. Do you have your key?" Eli asked, putting himself between the woman and the door.

"It's not locked." At his accusing look she hurried to add, "hey, we were right here! There was no way anyone could have gotten by us."

"Just wait here while I check it out." He let himself in after Tiny knocked him out of the way, bursting into the room. Eli closed the door behind him locking Danielle and Roxanna outside. They were left to stand and wait, worrying. After less than five minutes, Eli swung the door wide but stood blocking their way in.

"Okay. If I had to guess, I would say that you are normally a neat and tidy housekeeper..." he aimed the comment at Danielle.

"What's that supposed to mean?" She tried to push him out of the way to enter but he held her back.

"I'm guessing you had an uninvited visitor. The place is trashed. Somebody was looking for something." He stepped aside to let them enter and Danielle took one step inside then crashed to a halt, causing Roxanna to run into her from behind.

Danielle took in the scene with one slow scan. Pulled out drawers, tossed sofa cushions, open cabinet doors, and overturned furniture.

It was the feeling of having her private and personal space violated by a stranger that she couldn't tolerate.

Fear didn't reach her.

She was mad, spitting mad! Even Tiny could sense it and kept his distance.

When Danielle lowered her head, closed her eyes and started taking deep breaths to get some control, she felt Roxanna in front of her, hovering but not touching.

"Danielle? This guy is getting serious when he breaks into your home and does this. You aren't safe here anymore."

"Damn it! Don't you think I know that?" She struggled for control. She would not get emotional! Would not. Would. Not. "What else can I do? This is my home! I'm supposed to be safe here."

"Yes, but this is real bad."

"Who is this guy? What is he after?" Danielle realized she was clenching her teeth, fighting for control, and took a deep breath. Then another.

"I called your brother, he's on his way. Don't touch anything if you can help it. We might be able to pick up some fingerprints." She'd forgotten Eli was even in the room, her shoulders and neck tensed at the intrusion. "You need to pack a few things to last you a few days and you are moving in with me upstairs." When she started to refuse, he held up his hand. "It's no use arguing, your brother agrees with me. You have very few choices. You either move in with me or I move in with you here. The only other choice is that the hotel closes down until we catch this guy, for the safety of everyone here."

"But…"

"No buts. The dog can come along, if absolutely necessary."

"Danni, he makes a lot of sense." Roxanna interjected.

"My apartment has two bedrooms," Danielle said. "Roxanna can move in with me. I don't feel comfortable leaving her alone."

"Okay. So it's settled. Roxanna and myself are moving in with you as soon as Ben's men wrap up the scene and gather whatever evidence they can. We can help clean up when they're done."

"No, wait a minute! I said Roxanna can move in with me, there's no need for you here!"

"Actually, Danni," Roxie interrupted, "I'd prefer him here. I'd feel safer. Do you have a gun? A big gun?" she asked Eli.

"Well, yeah…"

"Do you know how to use it?"

"Of course, I do! I wouldn't be carrying a gun if I didn't know how to use it!"

"Okay, then. *Now* it's settled." Roxanna smiled. "Now, if you don't mind, I'm going to return to the front desk. You let me know when I should come over."

Danielle stared openmouthed at Roxanna's back as she left her alone with Eli, stunned at how she'd been manipulated.

"…and you!" She turned to Eli, wanting to vent on somebody and only finding him handy. "Who said you could have a gun in my hotel?"

"I didn't ask. I don't go anywhere without it. Ask your brother if you don't believe me."

"Ask me what?" Ben said from the doorway.

"Ben! Tell this…this…this…person! I am perfectly fine living here alone! I can take care of myself. I always have and always will!" She stomped her foot in aggravation as she caught the two men exchanging a look.

Eli crossed his arms at his chest, leaned back against the back of the sofa and silently waited for Ben to diffuse his sister's temper tantrum.

"Danni, give it up. You aren't going to win this argument. Consider Eli your best friend, at least for the time being. Between him and Tiny, you'll be living in Fort Knox."

"But…" Ben held up his hand, cutting off any arguments, just as Eli had done earlier.

"That's enough!" He snapped, putting an end to the conversation. "Okay, Eli. Tell me what happened."

And she was dismissed. Just like that! Just like a child. Well, okay. So maybe she was behaving a little like a child, but admitting it didn't make it any easier for her to accept. She stomped from the room and out to the office where she knew she could avoid everyone until she cooled down.

Tiny didn't follow this time.

****Chapter Eleven****

It was easy, really. She thought she was so clever hanging around the front lobby, like that would keep some-body - him - from getting into her apartment. Well, she didn't consider just how vulnerable her sliding glass door to the back patio was, especially since she never locked it.

Dumb broad.

He'd just had to get in there and find that camera be-fore she looked at those pictures of him, if she had any. It was one of those new digital contraptions that had a memo-ry card in it. He remembered seeing it when she was taking the pictures in the first place. It made a distinctive beeping noise when it took the picture.

He searched for the damned camera or even the mem-ory card and couldn't find it anywhere. Then he saw the camera bag hanging on the back of the doorknob of the bedroom door. He had already trashed the apartment look-ing for it, he was running out of time, she could come back to her apartment and catch him at any moment. He needed to get out of there.

Making a hasty decision, he grabbed the camera bag and dashed out the back door just as he heard the sounds of a barking dog.

Now where in the hell was barking coming from? The hotel didn't allow pets as far as he knew. So who had a dog...who was now barking...like crazy...from inside the hotel?

Well, he wasn't sticking around to find out. Running as fast as he could, he got out of there, ripping his pants on the outside door latch of the sliders as he escaped.

He ran to the nearby woods, gripping the camera bag in a death grip, afraid to drop it and lose the camera that he'd gone to all that trouble to get his hands on. When he'd made it a safe distance from the hotel, he dropped down in a pile of leaves to catch his breath and get a good look at the bag.

It felt kind of light, must be a lightweight camera to not weigh any more than what he held. He grasped the zip-per at the top of the bag and pulled it back to reveal its contents.

It was empty.

Damn it!

Damn damn damn!

Not only had he not found anything so he could end this frustrating game she was playing with him, now she'd have her guard fortified so he wouldn't be able to get anywhere near her or her apartment again. His messy search of the place had pretty much sealed that deal.

If only he'd found the camera! He would be able to go home and get back to his regular life.

A life with no stress.

A life with no other people to bother him.

A life where he is saving the world from all of its irritating life forms, like those now buried in these woods. His nice little growing collection of decaying life forms.

But, no!

He had to stay at this crummy hotel and pursue that crummy woman who had to have her crummy camera out taking crummy pictures the same day that he was getting rid of the crummy miserable bastard who, well, really deserved to be buried in that crummy grave in those crummy woods right now!

Now he had to come up with another plan.

And it had better not be a crummy one this time.

She couldn't sleep.

Her orderly life was out of her control. She'd spent too much of her life trying to get control of everything to let some nutcase come along and muck things up.

Tiny was snoring like a buzz saw at the foot of her king sized bed and she couldn't sleep. The only thing that helped when she couldn't sleep was a steaming mug of milk, preferably of the chocolate and spirits variety. Just thinking of spirits, she wondered where her friendly resident spirits had been keeping themselves lately. She hadn't seen or heard from Edna or Ruth for a couple of days now.

The thick cushion of the cut loop carpet felt good under her bare feet as she rolled out of bed and made her way to the kitchen. She slowed her steps to peek around the corner, hoping to avoid Eli. She didn't expect to find him sitting at her desk typing away at his laptop computer, clad only in dark blue pajama bottoms and snug Nike T-shirt.

With brow furrowed, pencil clasped in his teeth, his eyes were glued to the screen of his computer, pausing only to scribble something on a pad of paper then hop back on the keyboard and continue typing.

Her eyes wandered over him as he worked. His dark unruly hair had a tendency to curl around his face, one piece plopping across his forehead no matter how many times he combed it back with his hand. He really was a striking man, even with a day's growth of dark stubble and the whole finger-combed hair thing.

"Are you going to keep hiding back there or do you think you can come out and join me?" Eli had stopped typing and was lounging back in his chair with his hands clasped at his waist watching her.

"I couldn't sleep." Pushing away from the wall, she shuffled into the kitchen. "I thought I'd get something to drink." With shaking hands, she started banging cupboard doors open and closed while the supplies she was looking for seemed to be hiding from her.

"Here, let me do that." He'd crept up behind her to take the saucepan out of her hand and close the cupboard door. "You're making enough noise to wake the dead." He swung around at the sound of giggling behind him, but only found Danielle standing there, still refusing to meet his eyes. "What did you have in mind?"

"What?" After silencing the two naughty ghosts with a warning glare, she turned back to Eli. "Oh, I was going to heat up some milk. I can do it." She tried to grab the pan from him but he set it on the counter behind him and reached for her instead, spinning her around so her back was against the counter. He moved in close, trapping her in place with his hands bracketed on the countertop at either side of her hips.

"Maybe I know of some other way to help you sleep." He lowered his head as she waited, wanting to run but not able to move. Tilting her head back, she met his eyes - the bruise there a reminder of her violent actions from another day - before she felt the gentle persuasion of his lips touching hers. Was it guilt that held her in place? Why couldn't she make herself fight him or try to escape?

He took his time caressing her lips with his, her head thrown back under his gentle assault. One of his hands slid up her back, capturing and cradling her head as the other worked its way downward, pulling her hips in to meet his.

With shaky hands at his chest, she meant to push him away but instead felt them creep up around his shoulders, running her fingers through his thick hair to grasp him tightly at the back his neck, not wanting to let him go.

Arms tightened as his lips devoured hers, his tongue slipping past her lips, not letting her hide anything from him. His mouth left hers to scorch a trail of wild kisses across her neck and down her throat and back again, finally landing back on her hungry mouth, inhaling her moans as she felt his hands at her hips, lifting her to sit on the countertop in front of him. He spread her legs and fit himself in between, wrapping her legs around his hips, pulling her tightly around him.

She felt the burning heat of his hands as they lifted her nightshirt to touch her bare skin, and the old fear returned. Memories of another man, his kiss on her body, taking from her what she didn't want to give.

Everything in her froze, stiffening against him as she started to struggle, pushing at him, trying desperately to get away. As she raised one arm, prepared to strike out, she heard the low growl. Eli stepped back, catching her arm gently, his eyes on her face as he gave her some space but didn't release her completely.

Then the growling grew louder.

Reality crashed down on her like ice water when she realized who was growling.

It wasn't Eli.

Over Eli's shoulder she saw Tiny crouched in a menacing position, growling at the cowering figures of Ruth and Edna right before they disappeared.

Danielle slid off the counter, and shoved Eli out of the way, catching him off guard as she escaped into the living room, only then turning to face him.

He leaned back against the counter she'd just vacated,

crossing his arms over his chest, and faced her. He had questions, it was written on his face, but she wasn't in an answering mood.

Across the room, Tiny stood slobbering and wagging his tail, his stance non-threatening.

"What is it with this dog, anyway? Was he just growling at me?"

"…uh, yeah…he must have been growling at you. Probably thought he was protecting me or something." Danielle quickly covered. "That's a good little puppy."

"Damn dog," Eli said as he walked back to the living room, scratching Tiny behind the ears in passing.

"He's a good dog, he was protecting me." At the dark look Eli sent her, Danielle stuck out her chin and back-stepped into the hallway toward her bedroom.

He sat back down at his computer and started typing, effectively cutting her off. "Why don't you make yourself that cup of milk and go back to bed."

She hesitated for just a second before escaping to the safety of her bedroom.

Who did she need protection from, an unknown killer or Eli?

"Sister, I think we need to keep our eyes on this one,"

Edna whispered, watching Eli toss and turn on the sofa as he tried to sleep.

"Absolutely, Edna. He's a strong stubborn one, just what our Danielle needs. Maybe he just needs a little push from us occasionally in the right direction."

"Agreed, Ruth. He's already attracted to her, but Danielle won't be so easy. And we have to keep them safe, too."

"Yes, yes, yes. We'll just have to watch out for the dog, though. Who would have guessed that the beast would be able to see us?"

"Yes, who would have guessed?" Edna agreed. "But I think the dog will get used to us eventually. He just needs to get to know us, that's all. Once he does that, we'll get along famously."

"Yes, dear."

"I like to think we're likable."

"No doubt, sister. No doubt at all."

Eli rolled over on the couch and opened his eyes, searching the room, but he was alone.

"So, what have you got?" Wearing a path in Danielle's carpet with his pacing, Eli had his cell phone glued to his ear talking to Ben. Roxanna had gone to her apartment for a shower and Danielle was in her shower so he felt safe that he wouldn't be overheard.

"We have some information on the blood and those bullet casings."

"Great, where are you?"

"In town, at my office. How did last night go? Anything else happen that I should know about?"

"…not exactly…" Eli mumbled.

"What was that?"

"No, nothing. Quiet night."

"Well, that's good. So, you want to take a trip into town and see what we've got?"

Eli really needed to get away from the place for a couple of hours.

"While I was securing her patio doors I found a scrap of fabric snagged on the latch, I'll bring it with me. I'll just tell her I'm going in to town for those supplies for Thanksgiving."

"So how did the night go on her couch?"

"It wasn't really built for someone my size to be sleeping on. I may end up on the floor tonight." The chuckling at the other end of the line wasn't encouraging.

"I could help you drag a bed in there if this situation goes on for much longer, you know."

"I may hold you to that. Meanwhile, I'll catch you in town in about a half hour."

He disconnected and pocketed his phone as Danielle entered the room wrapped in a thick but well worn full-length robe. It didn't take a seasoned detective to figure out that she wore very little, if anything, under that robe.

"Are you trying to kill me here?" His eyes scorched a trail from her wet hair to the bare feet and slowly back up again, pausing on the bare skin exposed at her chest. His body was on instant alert and he felt that nervous twitch start in his left eye again.

"What?" she snapped. "What have I done now?"

"I'm going in to town for a while." Grabbing his car keys and jacket, he headed for the door. "You stay inside, don't even think about going outside the hotel. Don't venture anywhere within the hotel without Tiny. Stay in the office if possible. Find something to do to keep you busy in the office, anything. I don't care what, just don't do something stupid like take the dog outside. You hear me?" Spinning around to face her he waited for a reply. She silently nodded to his terse commands. "I'll be back before you know it. I'll pick up your supplies while I'm there. If you need anything else picked up, call me. I've left my cell number by your computer. Use it."

He walked out of her apartment without looking back.

"Look's like there was a hit on the DNA. That's a start." Ben studied the paperwork and the accompanying photograph. "Don't know that I recognize the guy. Mitch Bromley. Name's not familiar either. He look familiar to you?" He handed the picture to Eli, who shook his head then reached for the picture to get a closer look.

"Nope. Of course, he's bald in this picture and overly thin. It would be real easy to change your appearance just by growing your hair out and putting on some weight. From this we don't even know what his hair color is. Wait a minute, is this a military ID?"

"Hmm, says here he was briefly training with the Guard. That's how we were able to get it back so quickly. Didn't get far, though. Something about…oh, here it is. Shot himself in the foot. Was asked not to return. Seems he was a bit accident prone…on numerous occasions with loaded firearms."

"Well, that's interesting. That just might piss a guy off a little bit, don't you think?"

"I don't know if he'd go around in some small town trying to kill somebody though."

"Does this guy have an address around here, family or

friends familiar to this area. Is there anything to explain why he would even be around here?" Eli asked, trying to make some kind of connection but coming up blank.

"I don't see anything, but it only lists his last known address and that was the base."

"So, we're at a dead end."

"Maybe, maybe not. We have his DNA on file now, if we catch him on something else a red flag will pop up. Other than that I don't know. If I had a sketch artist around here I'd try to work up something with his picture, add some hair, see what he'd look like. Maybe we've seen him and just don't know it. I'll run the fingerprints we pulled at Danielle's apartment and see what we come up with. I still can't figure why he's after her."

"Who knows what goes on in the head of a psychopath. Maybe she was just in the wrong place at the wrong time." It was unlikely, but Eli was feeling helpless with the lack of clues about the guy. He'd known several criminals who effectively changed their appearance with tricks like hair color, weight loss or gain, or something as easy as a new wardrobe. Master chameleons. If that's what they were dealing with here, they had their work cut out for them in finding the guy.

"I'm going to run a check on this guy locally. I've

never heard of him but if he's from one of the surrounding towns he could easily have passed through here. Maybe we'll find he has family ties in the area."

"Sounds good. Can you get me a copy of this picture? I'm going to keep an eye out at the hotel, watch for anyone even resembling him."

"Yeah, and I think we should just keep this to ourselves until we know something more. No sense worrying the girls. I don't want Danielle feeling paranoid and living like she needs to watch over her shoulder all the time. Let's just handle this between us for now."

"Good plan. You can deal with her, though, when she finds out you've kept this from her." Eli agreed with a smile, already imagining the wrath Ben would face from his hot-headed sister.

"I'm not afraid of Danielle," Ben growled, then corrected himself, "well, maybe a little sometimes."

"I'm going to run over and pick up those supplies I promised her, and head back to the hotel. I still don't like being away for too long."

"Thanks. I appreciate you being there to handle things so I can watch things from here. I've looked after Danielle for most of her life, without her knowing of course. She's stubborn and really thinks she can take care of herself. I feel helpless not being able to watch over her right now with this going on."

"Hey, no problem."

"We really need to catch this guy. He could be hiding in plain sight and we wouldn't know it."

He didn't know what he'd find at the hotel that would help with the investigation, but keeping his eyes and ears open in the past had netted him many a bad guy.

It never failed.

Criminals either got sloppy, lazy, or cocky.

One of those would be this guy's undoing, Eli was sure of it.

Having a name helped to make the guy real.

Mitch Bromley.

At least that was the name he'd used when he'd been fingerprinted at basic training but it didn't help Eli with the real question; what was the guy doing here and why was he after Danielle? Everything that had occurred lately seemed to be aimed at Danielle or the hotel. This was all assuming the car accident, the bomb, the shooting and the break-in were all connected and it had all been the same guy involved. Eli didn't have anything to make that connection yet.

It was still a very real possibility that the guy was trying to suppress information she'd caught on her camera. Even though the search in the woods hadn't turned up anything, the scenario would certainly explain a lot.

Maybe it was time for him to take a walk in the woods for himself and take a look around.

Ah, there was that infernal vacuum cleaner out in the hallway signaling his nemesis at work.

How odd.

She'd been in hiding lately and now suddenly she's back to her regular routine around the hotel. That must mean she really didn't know anything about him or didn't feel threatened by him. Had he been worrying about nothing all this time?

Didn't matter.

He no longer cared whether or not she had pictures of him burying a body in the woods. Things had gone way beyond that now.

She had become a challenge.

He was determined to add her body to his collection.

She would not beat him. And maybe, just maybe, she was providing him his one last chance by teasing him out there in the hallway.

Having failed at the whole push-the-bitch-to-her-death-down-the-staircase thing before, he wouldn't fail this time. Most of the other guests were either away from the hotel or otherwise occupied in their apartments. The hotel was always deserted at this time of the day so nobody would be around to watch her limp dead body land at the foot of that horrible staircase. Just because he survived the fall down the staircase, didn't mean she would. It would be easy to haul her out to the trunk of his car without any witnesses. Her dead body belonged in the woods with his other trophies.

He giggled and peeked out his door to check on her. Sure enough, there she was coming around the corner with the vacuum roaring along in front of her.

Dumb broad.

She deserved to be thrown down the stairs.

She was practically begging him to do it and he would not disappoint her.

As she moved toward him, he closed his door, patiently waiting for her to pass and place herself at the top of the stairs.

He heard the roar of the machine.

Opening his door, he stepped out into the hallway.

He stayed behind her, out of sight.

Dash-at-her-and-push didn't work last time. This time he'd grab her and throw her.

It had to work.

He waited for his chance...waited for it...then, there it was!

He dashed at her with hands extended, counting on his superior size and strength to be able to pick her up. In slow motion, he imagined the feel of her in his hands, the soft weight of her body as he picked her up, the powerful feeling of tossing her down the staircase.

In his mind he could see and feel those things.

Things didn't happen the way he'd hoped.

Again.

When he was mere inches from reaching her he felt himself being physically picked up and thrown against the wall behind him, hitting the wall with such force it knocked the wind out of him. His body slid down the wall, landing in a stunned heap on the floor next to the door of his room.

Shaking his head, he looked up at the woman.

She couldn't possibly have done that. She hadn't even noticed him, just continued vacuuming with her back to him.

It was like she had some creepy force field around her!

She should be fearing for her life!

That was the way it was supposed to be!

Instead, here he was cowering in a miserable heap with another set of bruises forming, suddenly afraid for his life.

Every inch of his body was a galaxy of pain as he rolled onto his side toward his door and turned the doorknob. On hands and knees he crawled into his rented room, closing the door behind him with one foot.

Once inside he dropped to the floor, rolling onto his back and shuddering briefly before drowning in total body sobs.

"Did you see that, sister? He was trying to push her down the stairs!" Ruth asked. "If Vic hadn't come along when he did...well I hate to think what would have happened!" She fanned herself dramatically with one hand.

Vic leaned casually against the wall which had just been vacated, pleased with himself. It wasn't every day he got to be the hero, and he'd always wanted to try his strength on something other than just popping in and out.

"You ladies need anything else, you can count on Vic." He puffed out his chest.

"Thank you, Vic. I'm beginning to think the other

time wasn't just an accident. That man may have been trying to push her down the staircase that time, too!" Ruth exclaimed.

"I think so, too, sister. What are we going to do?" They looked to Vic for answers.

"There's no need to fear, ladies. Vic is here. I'm not going to let anyone hurt our Danielle. This guy clearly has bad intentions but he doesn't know who he's dealing with."

"We need to tell Danielle. She needs to know what just happened."

"Let's not rush into anything. Let me keep an eye on this clown, play with him a little bit and see what he's up to. If you tell Danielle, there's nothing she can do about it. She has no proof and she can't tell anybody that she got her information from a bunch of ghosts. Nah, leave it to me for now. Good old Vic is on the case. We'll make this guy sorry he messed with one of our family."

"Oh, I've always known Vic was such a good boy." Edna told her sister, who nodded in agreement.

"Now run along ladies. We don't want Danielle to see us and ask too many questions," Vic said as he passed through the door of the room where the injured man was hiding.

Like a cat with a mouse, he was going to enjoy playing with his new toy.

****Chapter Twelve****

With fingers to his mouth, Eli whistled for the dog, two short blasts. They'd been walking around the woods for about an hour and found nothing. Tiny had taken off to go do his business but Eli realized daylight was giving way to night. He needed to get back to the hotel before he ended up getting lost in these unfamiliar woods.

The clumsy crashing sound of big-dog-running-through-the-woods announced Tiny's arrival before he actually appeared. The slobbering-tail-wagging monster thundered from the brush and leapt out at him in excitement with something lodged in his massive drooling jaws.

"Ah, Tiny. What have you got there?" Eli tried to take it from the dog but rethought that plan when Tiny growled at him possessively. "Fine, keep it for now, but you aren't bringing it into the hotel when we get back." Shaking his head, Eli started the walk back to the hotel followed by Tiny who tripped over his big feet the whole way. Never having been an animal lover, Eli surprised himself in actually talking to a dog this way and enjoying the company of the sloppy awkward beast. "I don't know about you, buddy, but I'm starving." All he got in response from the dog was the same old ear-to-ear doggie grin and slobbery whole body tail wagging.

"You're so ugly you're cute. You're probably a hit with the ladies, huh?"

When they reached the turnaround in front of the hotel, Tiny ran ahead of Eli to wait at the front door. As Eli reached him he noticed that he'd abandoned his prize somewhere and was eagerly waiting to be let indoors, probably sensing dinnertime awaiting him.

Smart dog after all.

Tiny rushed past Danielle to Roxanna who took him back to the apartment to feed him, leaving Eli alone with Danielle.

She had one of those looks on her face, one that told him he wasn't going to like what she had to say.

"Do you remember asking me if anything was missing the other day when somebody broke into my place and I couldn't think of anything?" Eli nodded, slipping out of his jacket as he followed her to the apartment. "Well, something is missing. My camera bag."

"Okay, you're sure you didn't just put it somewhere and forget about it?"

"No. Look, I'm an organized person, a place for everything and everything in its place. It's gone."

"Let's not talk about this out here." He ushered her into her apartment, closing the door behind them to avoid being overheard. "Okay, so your camera is a target. Which means we're back to those pictures again."

"Bingo!" Danielle exclaimed.

"Calm down. I just walked way out into the woods to take another look around. I didn't see anything suspicious. Did anything happen around here today while I've been out?"

"Don't you think I would have told you if something happened around here! No! Nothing happened. I almost wish it would just so we'd have some clue to this guy, who he is and why he's doing this. I want my life back!" Danielle paced around her kitchen while Roxanna and Eli watched. They were interrupted by the ring tone of Eli's cell phone. Ben.

"Yeah." He answered it only after getting himself out of Danielle's earshot, to the living room.

"Hey, it didn't take me long to track down an address on Mitch Bromley. His last known was listed as his mother's house in the next town over, just on the other side of Danielle's woods."

"Is he still living there?"

"Well, now that's the thing. I sent a deputy to check it out. His car has been sitting in the driveway for several days but nobody has seen him coming or going. The other kicker; his mother has been missing for a few years now, he had her declared dead recently and collected on the inheritance and life insurance."

"You found out all this information just since I last talked to you?"

"Let's just say, he's not a real popular guy in his neighborhood. The neighbors were all eager to talk about the guy to men in uniform."

"Great. So what now?"

"Until we have an actual crime committed here I don't know."

"I still think we need to tighten up the security here at the hotel. I have a feeling the guy is escalating. He's getting sloppy. Danielle says her camera bag is missing, thinks it disappeared during the break in. That brings us back to those pictures."

"We need to take a closer look at those pictures."

"Agreed. Anything else?" Eli hoped for more to go on.

"Yeah, good luck up there. I know my sister can't be easy to live with right now."

"Ya think?" Eli agreed with a soft chuckle, sneaking a glance into the other room where Danielle was watching him with curious eyes. They locked eyes briefly before Eli turned away to resume his conversation with Ben in hushed tones.

"How's Tiny doing?"

"He's a handful, that's for sure. Say, if a person was to stop giving him water would that cut down on all that slobber?"

"Don't you dare mistreat my boy! So he slobbers a little bit, you just wait until you need him to catch a bad guy. He'll astound you."

"Yeah, I'll bet. He'd probably just sit on the guy."

"That is one of things Mastiffs are known for. Now, back to business. I'll follow up on these new leads and you try to keep my sister safe up there. Okay?"

"I'll do my best. If I don't end up strangling her myself," Eli mumbled.

"Not before Thanksgiving. I'm looking forward to a good home cooked meal next week. Try not to piss her off before then, will you?"

"Yeah. Look, I've got to go. She's heading over here with one of those looks. Catch up with me when you have something." He clicked his phone shut and slid it into his pocket as Danielle approached.

"Was that Ben?"

"Yup." He walked away from her to avoid questions, heading to the kitchen for something to eat. "What have you got around here to eat?"

"What did he have to say? Does he have any clues or anything?"

"Dunno." He continued rummaging through her cupboards and refrigerator, ignoring her questions. "How about some soup or something?"

He lay on the floor, trembling with aftershocks from what happened out in the hall. His sobs had exhausted him and he was having trouble dragging himself up off the floor so he stayed put. He didn't know how long he lay there, the vacuum had stopped long ago and she was gone. Could have been hours ago for all he knew.

The room had grown cold.

Refrigerator cold.

Deep-freeze cold.

He was freezing to death and couldn't get up off the floor to save his life! Rescue workers would probably find his frozen body days from now with a look of terror plastered to his face. Maybe at some point he would be able to curl up into a fetal position before he died, frozen like a Popsicle in this horrible room.

He had to get himself up.

Frost was forming on the windows and the sides of the furniture. His body trembled violently now, his teeth chattering so hard it made his head hurt.

Then he started hallucinating.

Rolling to his side and curling his body into a ball, he watched as the chair slid across the room toward him.

There was nobody there pushing it.

It just seemed to walk across the floor all by itself, stopping when it reached him then spinning around with its back facing him, then it just sat there.

His eyes rolled back into his head and everything went black.

The guy was a weasel. A weakling actually. You'd think he'd just seen a ghost or something.

Oh wait, maybe he had!

Vic straddled the chair he had positioned next to the

pathetic heap of man on the floor. He'd only just begun to play with the guy and he'd already passed out on him. Messing with him wasn't going to be much of a challenge. It would still be fun, the guy obviously was high strung and more than a little jumpy. Probably afraid of his own shadow.

Too bad.

Vic had hoped to get a little more play out of him. Disappointing.

Oh well.

He'd just sit and wait for him to wake up, he had nowhere else to go.

Later he'd move some things around in the apartment, throw something, make some chain rattling sounds, some moaning and groaning.

All typical ghost stuff.

Scare the guy a little, see what he was made of.

Vic was looking forward to the game.

The guy had tried to push Danielle down a flight of stairs.

He felt compelled to teach the guy a lesson.

****Chapter Thirteen****

Eli had just drifted off to dreamland when something dragged him back.

The stale, pungent odor of drooling doggie jowls, up close and personal.

Still on the edge of sleep, he reached up to wipe at his face. When his hand came away dripping with wet ooze he was instantly awake, staring into big brown puppy eyes less than an inch in front of him.

He sat up, silently cursing the dog that was watching his movements. A whine squeezed out of Tiny and he swung his head to look down the hallway toward Danielle's bedroom then back at Eli.

Pushing himself up off the couch, Eli walked into the kitchen to splash some water on his face and clean his gooey hand. When he looked back at Tiny, the dog swung his head toward the bedroom.

"Okay. I get it. You want me to follow you, right?" Eli asked, finding it hard to believe he was having this conversation with a dog. That didn't stop him from following Tiny to Danielle's bedroom.

When they reached the spot outside her open doorway and heard the sounds of a struggle, he burst into her bedroom expecting to find her being attacked by an intruder.

Danielle was fighting off an invisible attacker and begging for help. The covers were twisted around her sweaty body and her arms stiff at her sides as though being held prisoner by unseen hands. Her head swung from side to side so close to hitting the headboard that Eli rushed forward to wake her before she hurt herself.

"Danielle? Wake up!" Her body rolled toward him as he sat on the edge of the bed. Grabbing her by the arms and pulling her upright, he shook her lightly when she didn't wake right away. "Danielle! You're having a nightmare. Wake up."

With an anguished cry, she went limp in his hands and he released her back on the mattress, exhausted. When her eyes opened she saw his form sitting on her bed and swung one arm at him, but he caught her hand before it hit him in the face, pulling her into his arms in an attempt to calm her down.

"Shh, Danielle. It's Eli. You were having a nightmare. You're awake now. You're safe. Nobody's going to hurt you, I'm right here, you're safe." He massaged her back, as though taming a wild animal, until she calmed and relaxed in his arms. When she started trembling, he pulled up the blanket and wrapped it tightly around her body, lifting her into his lap as he turned to sit on the bed with his back against the headboard, hugging her close to the warmth of his body until her trembling eased. He tucked her head under his chin and she burrowed her slim body into the curve of his.

This wasn't just any nightmare.

He'd been a cop long enough to recognize the reactions of an assault victim when he saw them.

Grinding his teeth, his mind flashed to an ugly picture, Danielle fighting for her life, a monster forcing her, attacking her, violating her.

Then everything came into focus.

Always hiding that luscious body behind baggy clothes and bib overalls.

Her defensive behavior, skittishness around him, tough attitude, stubborn determination to be independent, strike-first-ask-questions-later attitude.

Her need to avoid contact with other people – except her brother. Roxanna handled most of the direct contact with the guests of the hotel. He hadn't even realized it until now.

Her brother.

Ben probably knew about the attack and had been protecting her. The threats to kick his ass if he touched her…those weren't idle threats.

He lost track how long he'd held her before he realized she had fallen into a calm relaxed sleep. Sliding down on the mattress, he wrapped himself around her and pulled the blanket up around both of their bodies.

He'd deal with her temper in the morning but for tonight he wasn't leaving that bed. He was right where he wanted to be and he'd worry about the consequences later. As he drifted off to sleep, he felt Tiny join them, settling himself - after a couple of circling motions - at the foot of the bed and snoring as soon as his head hit the mattress.

"I have to go home for Thanksgiving. My aunt died. Mom needs me to say her goodbyes." Roxanna was cramming clothes into a small soft-sided suitcase. It was four days before Thanksgiving, Danielle was hiding from a possible killer, and now she had to handle it all without her best friend.

"You need to be there for your mom, tell her all the things she wants to hear." Danielle reassured the other woman when what she really wanted to do was beg her to stay.

"Yeah."

"Hang in there. Did you know your aunt very well?" Danielle watched as Roxanna hitched the shoulder strap over her shoulder.

"Never met her. She and Mom fought a lot."

"Well, I'll feel better about you getting away from this place right now, anyway. I hate putting everybody in danger, I hope this is over soon. Ben and Eli don't tell me anything about the investigation, but I know something is going on. They have this big male ego thing going on, chest thumpers protecting the female. The big dumb apes!"

"Let it go, Danni. Ben needs to feel like he's protecting you. He still feels guilty about your step dad."

"I don't know why. None of it was Ben's fault."

"He's your big brother. Give him a break."

"Fine. Now, get going before it gets dark out." Danielle hugged her quickly then pushed her out her apartment door, following her to the front of the hotel and watching until her taillights faded around the curve of the driveway.

Tiny whimpered beside her, sensing her mood.

"Come on, boy. Let's go get you something to eat before big bad Eli joins us for the night and crashes our fun."

"Hey, I heard that," Eli said from the staircase as he reached the bottom. "Have you locked up? Or you want me to do it?"

"I've already locked up. Roxie just left."

"Is she going to call you to let you know she made it safely?" .

"Yeah. I was just going to feed Tiny." Danielle walked ahead of Eli to her apartment, dragging her feet, blaming him for her bad mood. Tiny had already run ahead of her and was waiting at the door, his wagging tail thumping the door in excitement as he watched and waited for her.

"I'll just double check everything and be right there."

"Sure, whatever."

Eli smiled at her cranky mood, remembering the time spent in her bed the night before. He'd waken early and left while she slept. She'd been lying across his hard body with one leg wrapped around his thighs, her hand flat on his lower abdomen. It took every ounce of willpower he possessed to pry her hands from his body, climb from the bed, and leave the room, his aroused body screaming in protest.

From her attitude this morning, he suspected she didn't remember anything from their night together.

Not something a man finds particularly flattering when a woman doesn't remember sleeping with him, but with this woman he counted himself lucky for her memory lapse.

The day had passed uneventfully. They hadn't had any additional attacks or incidents. That worried him.

The break in of her apartment suggested the guy was escalating and becoming sloppy, but then all activity stopped.

Had he found what he was looking for? Or was he just taking a break and regrouping?

If the guy was just regrouping, the next action he took could be big. The hotel full of people could be targets or unwitting pawns in the guy's game. If he really was a psychopath there was no telling how far he'd go to complete his task.

Was the guy willing to risk his own life for the cause?

Eli finished checking all the windows and doors.

Time to head back to Danielle's apartment.

They'd be alone tonight.

It would be a long night.

When he entered, Danielle was nowhere in sight and he guessed she'd gone to her room to sulk with Tiny as her eager sidekick.

That worked fine for him. He could get some writing done. She was becoming a constant distraction and didn't even need to be in the same room with him.

****Chapter Fourteen****

When he dragged himself up off the floor, his quiet apartment looked normal. The chair was where it belonged at the desk across the room. Everything was right where he'd put it, nightclothes laid out on the bed, his other clothes hanging neatly in the open closet.

He must have dreamed the whole episode of the night before and spent a long miserable night curled up on the cold floor, too scared to get himself to the bed where a nice warm blanket was calling him.

What had happened to him?

With one hand he felt along his ribs then moved his hand as far as he could reach on his back, pulling it away quickly as he touched on what he was sure were badly bruised ribs. Did he get that from sleeping on the floor?

No.

Then it came back to him.

The whole violent scene in the hallway where the girl had somehow thrown him against the wall when he'd snuck up on her from behind.

He'd been caught by surprise.

Who would have guessed that little slip of a girl would have such strength?

She was tall but thin...and she was a girl!

Girls don't throw people across the room!

Did they?

He'd do good not to underestimate her again.

Creeping his way to the bathroom and the awaiting shower, he peeled the clothes from his weary body as he went along, hissing in pain as each layer was removed. In the bathroom, he checked his naked body in the mirror. If he didn't have such an important job to complete, his body was telling him he should be lying in a hospital bed reco-vering from all of his wounds right now. His torso was a canvas of black and blue, front and back, with matching bruises along both arms and legs. So far, his face had been spared any marks so he would be able to hide the injuries from any nosy people, but he didn't know how long that would last at the rate he was going.

The scar on his foot where he'd shot himself was bare-

ly detectable under multiple bruises and skin scrapes.

While he checked himself in the mirror, he let the shower warm up, filling the room with soothing steam.

Easing into the shower one leg at a time, he pulled the shower curtain closed behind him, relaxing under the hot spray of water, letting it wash away the tension and disappointments of the day.

The hot temperature that had lulled him into relaxation suddenly turned ice cold, jerking him back to attention and sending him stumbling from the shower stall, ripping the shower curtain from its rod as it wrapped around his naked body and tripped him, dumping him on the floor. He peeled the curtain from his face as he tried to catch his breath and something drew his attention to the steam-fogged mirror.

His terrified brain read the words being spelled into the steam, as though written by an invisible finger, sending him a message from beyond.

YOU ARE A DEAD MAN!

He scrambled across the bathroom floor to get away, slamming the door behind him as he made it into the other room, dragging himself to the farthest corner of the bedroom, still wrapped in the clinging shower curtain. Cowering in the corner of the bedroom, he watched as the bath-

room door opened, letting the steam billow out, framing a man's form in the mist. As the steam dissipated, so did the man's form so that he wasn't sure he'd even seen it in the first place.

He let out the breath he'd been holding and passed out.

Vic watched as the man passed out on him again. Disgraceful. He wasn't much fun if he was going to keep passing out on him.

He was pretty proud of that whole mirror-writing thing though.

Truly inspired.

Maybe being a ghost wasn't such a bad thing after all. After decades of hanging around the old hotel he was finally having some fun.

If only this guy were more of a challenge.

Too bad.

He pulled up the chair and straddled it again, waiting for the guy to wake up, planning his next move.

If the guy didn't die from a heart attack first.

Eli was up before Danielle so he let Tiny out for his morning business. As soon as the door was open, Tiny was off and running into the woods. The sounds of him crashing through the trees and underbrush echoed back to Eli where he stood at the front of the hotel.

While Tiny was off on his run, Eli decided to take a look around the outside of the hotel, scanning for anything that didn't look right. Walking around the perimeter of the hotel, checking in bushes and watching for footprints or signs that somebody may have been sneaking around outside, he came up empty.

Why had nothing happened for several days now? The guy had started out with mischief just about every day and now nothing. What had happened to shut the guy down? And was he actually shut down?

Eli returned to the front of the hotel to wait for Tiny. When the dog didn't return right away, he whistled and called his name. Within seconds the dog pounded toward him in the brush, loping out of the wooded area and into the clearing.

Again, Tiny had a prize clasped in his big mouth. Eli couldn't tell what it was and forgot about it when Tiny dropped it by the rose bushes at the side of the hotel to follow him indoors.

Danielle had already warned Eli that she would be baking pies and working on other preparations all day for their Thanksgiving dinner so he would need to find something to keep him busy and keep Tiny out of her way in the kitchen. He planned to write all day, originally in his room, but something made him set up his laptop in her living room instead.

His gut was telling him he needed to keep an eye on Danielle, to stay close. He still wasn't sure she was out of danger.

Something in his chest told him he just wanted to keep an eye on her for other reasons. Maybe it was that oversized apron telling him to kiss the cook, which he ached to do. Maybe it was the way she measured ingredients together in her mixing bowl, detailed, organized and precise. Each mixing spoon, cup, spatula and knife was lined up on the counter in front of her, nothing out of place.

Her long brown hair was pulled back in a ponytail but several tendrils had worked loose to hang in her face as she worked. He knew that had to drive her crazy, it was driving him crazy.

Her hands were kneading each pile of dough with care, her perfect kitchen spotless even as she was working.

He'd never met a neat-and-tidy cook. How she managed to keep everything so clean while working was a mystery.

They had reached a companionable truce for the day and he almost missed fighting with her. They weren't arguing…or anything…and she seemed to be ignoring him.

He didn't like it much.

He was having problems concentrating on his work. The more she fought to push him away, the more he craved any moment he could spend in the same room with her.

Tiny lay beside him on the floor, having been banished from the kitchen after an ugly pie eating incident earlier. He was whining as though he were in pain, slobbering himself into a puddle so bad that Eli had to slip a towel under his snout to catch the drool.

Eli was guessing Tiny was an apple pie man like himself but, boy, that pumpkin pie sure smelled good, too.

It was hopeless.

There was no way he'd be able to concentrate on his work so he closed down his laptop and joined Danielle in the kitchen, leaning on the counter at the far end where he could watch but stay out of her way. Tiny followed him to the edge of the kitchen and parked himself there, having already had the kitchen boundaries firmly explained to him.

"So, Danielle." Eli opened the conversation, but paused, realizing he'd startled her as she jumped and swung around on him. "Tell me a little bit about the people who live here. Give me an idea who's going to be joining us for dinner tomorrow. I'd also like some information so we can rule each of them out as suspects."

"Well, not much to tell." As she listed her guests, mentally going from room to room, he caught an occasional smile for the people she obviously liked better than others. When she stopped talking, he realized she'd come around to him.

"Who else?"

"Well you, of course, in 2H and Wally Parker in 2F. You both checked in within a few days of each other. We don't see Mr. Parker very much. Not a very social kind of guy. Comes and goes, doesn't talk to any of the other guests. Roxie checked him in and I've only seen him maybe once or twice, harmless looking enough."

"Why do you say that?"

"I don't know, just a feeling. Kind of a geek. Looks like he probably spends most of his time with his nose in a book or playing video games. You know, has that never-goes-outdoors pallor. Probably has a collection of bugs at home." Tapping her finger on her chin, she hesitated before continuing. "We have a few rooms empty on the second and third floors right now. People come and go with the seasons and Holidays. We have regulars who will be back at New Year's and in the spring."

"I'm only concerned about those that are staying here right now."

"Why? Do you really think any of them could be responsible for the violent act of shooting at somebody? Or a bomb? What about running me off the road?" She was punctuating her words with her chopping knife then slapped it down on the counter with horror on her face, obviously just realizing she'd been waving it at him.

"We can't rule anybody out right now except maybe Roxanna and the two of us, and Ben, of course. What about the people in town? Can you think of anyone there that might have a bone to pick with you or the hotel?"

"No, we're good for business. The hotel brings in customers and keeps them in business. Besides, the Manchester has been here for generations. The town survives because of it. Who would mess with that?"

"Then it must be personal. We keep coming back to those pictures. Too bad we can't see anything on them, but the bad guy doesn't know that, does he?" That gave him an idea.

"Eli?" Ignoring her, he walked back into the living room, his cell phone already at his ear. "Oh, great! More secret talks with my brother!" She muttered and turned back to her cutting board. "Men! Like I need you to take care of me…" she continued mumbling and hacking away at the helpless apples on her cutting board.

Eli concentrated on his call, but kept her in his sights.

She was wielding the big knife, again, after all.

A wise man didn't turn his back on an angry woman with a knife.

"Honey, what are you so worried about? Don't you want somebody else to take care of things once in a while?" Danielle jumped as Edna's voice spoke from beside her. Ruth was standing with her but watching Eli across the room.

"No, I was doing just fine before he came along." Danielle turned back to the counter, keeping her head down so Eli wouldn't hear her talking and start asking questions. He didn't seem like an I-live-with-ghosts-and-am-not-afraid-to-tell-people-about-it kind of guy.

"Nonsense, sweetie. It's nice to have somebody to worry about you. Somebody besides us, of course," Ruth piped in, "and watch what you're doing to those apples. You're not going to have anything left but mush for the pies if you keep chopping them like that."

"Sorry, Ruth." She scraped the pieces into a bowl and

reached for the next batch to chop. "He and Ben are trying to run my life and I don't like it."

"Well, in my day women liked to be taken care of by a big strong man and he seems to be a very nice man. And your brother loves you very much. Be nice," Edna scolded.

"Yes, Edna…"

"What? Did you say something?" Over her shoulder, she saw Eli set his cell phone on the counter and walk back into the kitchen. Ruth and Edna disappeared as he passed through them. "Brrr! It suddenly got cold in here. Is this place drafty or something?" He tried to sneak a piece of chopped apple from her bowl but snapped his hand back when she threatened him with the knife. His hands went up in mock surrender as he backed away from her.

"So, Ben will be here early in the morning to help set up for the dinner. Is that the plan?"

"I don't know, why didn't you ask him when you had him on the phone?" She flashed him a not-so-innocent smile and turned back to her work, the knife slamming the cutting board with each chop.

Hoping he would take the hint and leave the room, she didn't expect him to sneak up on her and slide his hands down her arms from behind, smoothly removing the knife from her hand to set it safely on the counter out of her reach. When his arms wrapped around her waist and pulled her back against his hard body, all thoughts of struggling abandoned her. His face dropped to her neck, blazing a trail of slow melting kisses across the back of her neck and around to where her neck met her shoulder, nudging her head to the side to allow him access.

Her brain was screaming at her to step away...tell him to stop...protest...anything but this, but her body went limp, inviting his lips to explore further.

Was this what a strong independent woman would do? Let a man take complete control of her weakening body? Her senses? She only knew that she didn't have control of her body or her senses whenever he was near. When he touched her, she instantly melted and became putty in his arms, his hands. A tortured moan escaped her when one of his hands lowered to the subtle swell of her belly, sliding to her core, pulling her tightly back against his hardness, throbbing against her back.

He growled and spun her around in his arms, his mouth crashing down on hers, devouring her as he pressed her back against the counter. Her head was spinning out of control and she gripped his arms, afraid she'd crumple to the floor if she didn't hang on to him for support. His hands grasped her backside and pulled her into himself, leaving her no doubt that he was ready for action.

The ringing of the oven timer brought reality crashing in. Wedging her hands between them, she tried to push him away, frantic that things had gone too far.

"Eli, we have to stop! Please! Eli!"

He pulled his face from hers and eased his body only far enough away for him to rest his forehead against hers, breathing deeply, sucking in ragged breaths.

"Eli. Let me go. Please." Danielle pried herself out of his arms and stepped away from him, her heart thundering in her chest. He still held her loosely in his arms, his dark gaze capturing her nervous one, apparently not yet ready to let her go. One hand reached up to caress the loose hair from her face where it had escaped the ponytail and fell to her chin, lifting her face so he could drop one last lingering kiss on her lips before stepping away from her and dropping his hands.

"This isn't over, Danielle." His hot fudge eyes poured over her like molten lava, melting her as the caressing tone of his voice sent a new set of trembles traveling through her body.

He pulled his hand roughly through his hair and the sight of his shaking hand mirrored how Danielle was feeling at the moment. Turning away from her he grabbed his cell phone and stalked out of the apartment, not looking back.

****Chapter Fifteen****

Ben arrived at the hotel early on Thanksgiving morning to help set up tables and go wherever his help was needed. Eli was passing through the hotel lobby as he came in the front door.

"Hey," Ben mumbled at him as he entered, Eli mumbled back as he obeyed Danielle's instructions and headed for the basement to haul tables and chairs up to the front lobby where they would be eating.

"I can't tell you how good it is to have another guy here to do all of her grunt work," Ben said and followed Eli to the basement. "It's usually just me and then I'm exhausted by the time the food is on the table. She's a hard task master."

"Yeah, so I'd gathered. It's still dark out and she's got us doing manual labor."

"Uh huh. But once you sink your teeth into one of her pies you'll know it's all been worth it." Eli was envisioning his teeth on something else of Danielle's and nodded at Ben's words, agreeing that it would be worth it.

"Anything new on that Bromley guy?" Eli brought up the subject, not sure if he wanted to hear the answer. They needed to catch the guy before he hurt somebody…if he hadn't already.

"If this guy's in the area, it's only a matter of time before he's going to do something stupid and we'll be there to catch him."

"Something stupid like sticking a homemade bomb in a dumpster, or running himself into a ditch and leaving a trail of his blood behind as evidence. Or…I know…breaking into Danielle's apartment and only stealing an empty camera case? Everything he's done, so far, has been incredibly stupid." Eli was feeling punchy.

"Okay, I mean something even more stupid than what he's done so far. And I'm still thinking about your idea about drawing the guy out with hints about the pictures, but I'm not real fond of the idea of offering my sister up as bait to some nutcase obsessed with her."

Eli's obsession with Danielle was what had gotten him involved in the investigation in the first place, but he wasn't about to admit anything to Ben at the moment. He didn't think he'd need to. Ben was studying him with a speculative gleam in his eye.

Eli turned away, avoiding the sharp eye of his fellow lawman, fully appreciating the conflict of interest he was mired in if he were to get involved with the man's sister.

"So, where are these tables we're supposed to be hauling up?" Eli quickly changed the subject. With a slight hesitation, Ben pointed him in the direction he needed.

"Don't think I'm not aware of your interest in my sister and don't underestimate me if you hurt her." Ben warned as they each grabbed a table and headed for the stairs. "I may seem mild mannered and easy to get a long with, but where my sister is concerned, there's nothing I wouldn't do to protect her."

"Good to know." Eli acknowledged with a nod. Eyeing the local lawman, he guessed any fight that might erupt between them would leave him the loser. Eli was tall and fit but Ben had him beat by a couple of inches and at least twenty extra pounds of muscle. Ben could probably wrestle a grizzly bear and win. "And I assure you, we're on the same page. I'll do everything in my power to keep her from getting hurt."

"Good. I'd hate to have to kick your ass."

"Again, good to know. Not real fond of the idea, my-self. Always prefer not to be on the receiving end of an ass kicking." Eli agreed and they relaxed again, the tension of the moment eased. As they reached the top of the stairs, Eli stopped Ben to ask a question that had been bothering him.

"I have to ask. You don't have to answer if I've over stepped my bounds, but it may have some bearing."

"Okay. But I'm already not liking the sound of it." Ben set his table down and turned to face Eli.

"Just so I'm up to speed at the dinner table, what's the story with you and Danielle? How did she happen to end up here, inheriting this hotel and its odd collection of occu-pants?"

"Well, I'd really feel more comfortable with you ask-ing her those questions, but knowing Danielle, she won't tell you much."

"Yeah, that's what I'm guessing."

"You know she left home when she was sixteen, right?"

"Ran away from home is the way I heard it."

"Okay. Yeah, she ran away from home. I was finish-ing up at school so I wasn't around much."

"Let's cut to the chase. She's having some pretty wicked nightmares." Eli set his table down and waited for

Ben to start talking, he sensed the inner struggle the other man was dealing with.

"I wonder when those started again, probably the stress of what's been happening around here lately," Ben muttered, shaking his head. "God. She'd been doing so good."

"Tell me," Eli insisted.

"Not much to tell." Ben grimaced, rubbing the back of his neck before talking. "Bad childhood. Worthless mother. Stepfather." Ben talked as he set up his table then took Eli's and assembled it, keeping his hands busy. "I was twenty, Danielle fourteen. He had a taste for teenaged girls. Then Danielle turned sixteen." A look of sick fury came over Ben's face and Eli didn't need to hear the rest, nausea and rage filled him, mental images telling him the story.

"Where is the guy?"

"In Washington. I can't touch him. I've tried."

"Could this guy be here, now?"

"I don't think so, I've tried to keep tabs on him, know where he is at all times."

"So, he's probably not our guy…"

"Probably not. And for the record…we never had this conversation." At Eli's nod, Ben changed the subject. "Let's finish setting this up so Danielle can get this party started. I've been dreaming about her apple pies for weeks now."

"I'm right there with you. I had to suffer through the baking process yesterday. She threatened me and Tiny if we came anywhere near the kitchen. I don't take her threats lightly when she's wielding a big kitchen knife."

The tables had been set up end to end with chairs on both sides for everyone to gather as one big family. This was the part Danielle enjoyed the most, when she got to spend time with her guests, visit with them and hear about their lives and memories. Most stories she'd heard several times from those who were long time residents of the hotel, but she always enjoyed hearing the stories since her own family life was not filled with happy memories.

Roxanna had called with well wishes and Danielle was missing her, this would be the first Thanksgiving they had spent without each other in almost ten years. The other women of the hotel were helping her carry the food in from her apartment and arranging it on the tables with the men handling the heavier dishes, including the large turkey platter.

When all had been transported to the tables, they took their seats. Ben sat near Danielle at one end of the tables and Eli took the other end facing her, the spot usually occupied by Roxanna.

Danielle reached for Ben's hand beside her, who interlaced his fingers with hers, as she spoke to her guests.

"I just wanted to take a minute to welcome you all to this table. This is my opportunity to show how much I appreciate all of you. Thanks for being here. Enjoy yourselves. I especially want to say how thankful I am for my brother, Ben." Then turning back to her guests, she said, "Now, enough with all the mushy stuff. Let's eat!"

She spared a glance to the other end of the table as the sound of conversation and the activity of the feast warmed her. Eli's eyes glowed back at her across the length of two tables and the flames of his stare sent a melting heat down her body, promising things she wasn't sure she could handle.

She refused to meet his eyes again.

At one point she raised her eyes to find Ruth and Edna standing at the front counter with Sebastian. Vic was standing behind one of her guests watching him eat...that Wally fellow.

Why would Vic be so interested in the new guy?

And why was Mr. Parker glaring at her like that?

****Chapter Sixteen****

Well, wasn't this just FREAKING fantastic!

One big happy family gathered around the happy happy happy dinner table! Just like life on FREAKING Walton's Mountain!

What was he thankful for?

He was thankful he was still alive, for one thing, after the night he'd just spent dodging flying objects in his haunted room upstairs. He didn't know what he'd done to make some ghost want to torture him but that's what was happening.

And there SHE was...sitting at the head of the table acting as though nothing had happened lately. Shouldn't she be acting scared for her life or something? Was she not taking him seriously? Maybe it was time for him to take things up a notch, not that he hadn't been trying. Some-

thing always seemed to be getting in the way of him taking care of business.

The sooner he took care of the broad, the sooner he could return to his safe world away from all these obnoxiously happy people. He stared down the table, across the expanse of talking people. People totally ignorant of the fact that he would happily take any one of their lives and bury them in the woods.

She was daintily picking at her food in between conversations with the people sitting near her...laughing!

Disgusting!

Unaware of the danger she was in at any given moment.

He was a force to be reckoned with!

She should be cowering in fear! Afraid for her life! And here she was partying with a bunch of weirdoes eating turkey!

He watched her, his eyes burning with hatred as he reached for his fork but came up with empty tablecloth. Looking away from her for a minute to locate his fork, he watched in horror as the fork lifted in the air and stabbed into his hand, skewering it to the table.

His scream shattered the quiet table conversation and silence filled the room as all eyes swung to look at him, blood pouring from the wound in his hand, staining the nice white linen tablecloth.

The pain!

Oh. My. God.

The pain!

Nothing that he'd endured, nothing that had happened to him, nothing since moving into this shit-hole of a hotel was as horrible as the pain right now!

He passed out, slumping in his chair, held upright only by the fork that pinned his hand to the table.

Danielle caught a glimpse of Vic backing away from the man before disappearing, then focused on Wally Parker where he slumped in his chair at the table. Stunned for a minute, the roomful of people hesitated before Eli and Ben jumped up from their chairs and ran to Wally's side.

She searched for Ruth and Edna, looking for answers, but they only shrugged and faded out.

Sebastian hissed, hunched up his back and was gone.

Ben reached the man first, grabbing several napkins the other guests pushed at him to wrap around the man's bleeding hand. When Eli reached his side, the two of them grabbed the fork and pulled it out of his hand, catching the man's body before it slumped to the floor.

"Danielle, call Hank Sommers at home. Tell him what's happened and get him here as soon as possible!" Ben barked, but Danielle was already on the phone to the local volunteer fireman and EMT. Ben and Eli lowered Mr. Parker's body to the floor and tried to stop the bleeding. "...and can somebody get us a blanket or something to cover him up before he goes into shock?"

It wasn't until the man's hand was firmly wrapped and the blanket was tucked around him that Ben stopped to assess the situation.

"What the hell just happened here?" he asked. Getting no response, he asked again. "Did anybody see what happened? Who would have stabbed this guy with a fork?"

The room was filled with faces of confusion.

Danielle felt helpless, she knew something but couldn't tell anybody. Where was Roxanna when she needed her?

"Did this guy stab himself with his own fork?"

"Sheriff." One guest interrupted him. "I was sitting right next to him and I didn't see anything. He's one of those people that you just don't pay any attention to, like he's invisible or something. One minute we're all eating and talking then the next minute he's shrieking and has a fork in his hand! Nobody was there. He had to have done it himself, we would have seen somebody."

"That's right, Sheriff. I was sitting on the other side of him. One minute everything is fine and then the next, this."

"Maybe he's suicidal or something…" Suddenly all of her guests were talking and agreeing. "He never talks to anybody, not in a rude way or anything, he just doesn't want anything to do with anybody. Just keeps to his room all the time, never speaks to you when you pass him in the hallway or anything. I've tried and he looks away and avoids me. The last couple of days there have been some strange noises coming from his room. Was he trying to kill himself or something?"

"Well, he'll be taking a trip to the hospital for now. We can talk to him later. Nasty injury, though. Going to take more than a couple of stitches to fix him up." As Ben was talking, the crunch of gravel announced a vehicle pulling up to the hotel. "Hopefully, that's the EMT's, Danielle?"

"I'll go get them." Danielle ran for the front door, glad to have something to do.

She was the only one present who knew Mr. Parker hadn't stabbed himself.

She needed to talk to Vic.

Unfortunately, he'd disappeared and wasn't in any

hurry to make another appearance. In fact, none of her ghosts were present. A nagging feeling was creeping down her spine, something bad was going on and she needed to get some information and quick.

"Right this way, Hank. He's bleeding real bad and has been unconscious for a half hour now." She held the door for the EMT as he and his partner wheeled a gurney into the hotel lobby with medical bags and equipment loaded on top. She'd given them detailed information about the situation when she'd called so they were prepared for anything. Ruth, Edna and Vic remained stubbornly absent. It looked like she would be on her own on this one, especially since she had to let Ben and Eli keep thinking the guy had stabbed himself.

They wouldn't believe the truth.

A ghost had stabbed one of her guests and she had no idea why.

"I'm going to follow the paramedics to the hospital and see what I can find out about his condition. I'll call you when I have something." Ben reassured Danielle and Eli as he lowered himself into his car. "Don't worry. It was just a freak accident, Danni. It had nothing to do with you or the hotel. As soon as he wakes up, I'll get some answers and this will all blow over." He shut his door, buckled himself in and waved at them as he backed out to follow the emergency vehicle.

"Come on, let's try to salvage your delicious Thanksgiving dinner." Eli nudged her. She fell into step beside him as they returned to the hotel. Inside, the others had done the best they could at cleaning up the mess. They'd stripped the table of the unsalvageable heirloom tablecloth and reset everything, knowing how important the dinner was to Danielle.

She forced a smile in thanks and dropped her suddenly weary body in the chair at the head of the table. Eli took Ben's chair. The food had grown cold but they ate as though it was the best meal they'd ever feasted on. She only picked at her food, but tried to put on a brave face for her guests.

Tiny would enjoy a mighty Thanksgiving dinner of leftovers that night, but Danielle had some ghosts to worry about.

"So, how's our patient?" Eli asked Ben when he called to check in later that evening.

"He spent several hours in surgery. The surgeons had to reattach tendons and repair some shattered bones. They doubt he'll ever regain full use of that hand."

"Did he ever wake up enough to talk to you?"

"Nope. I'll try again tomorrow. I did talk to the doctor who worked on him in the emergency room and then the surgeon. Funny thing. They both agreed that the guy looked like he'd been worked over pretty bad, mostly recent stuff but also older injuries that hadn't healed yet."

"What kind of injuries?" Eli asked, intrigued and more than a little alarmed at the news.

"Heavily bruised over most of his body. When they were prepping him for surgery, they cut his bloodied clothing off him and found bruising - possibly as recent as twenty four hours - and they suspect some broken ribs as well as sprains and cuts that haven't been allowed to heal. The guy had to be a walking bundle of constant pain. No wonder he passed out at the table, this wasn't his first injury."

"You think somebody's been roughing him up since he moved in to the hotel."

"Won't know until I get a chance to question him." Ben yawned at the other end of the phone and Eli realized how little sleep the lawman must have been getting lately.

"Why don't you go home and get some rest. I'd like to be there when you return to the hospital to talk to him."

"Yeah, I left notice with the hospital to call me as soon

as the guy is awake. Hopefully, that'll happen tomorrow. I'll bet they have him drugged up pretty good for the night."

"Great. Let me know and I can meet you there." Eli's instincts were on high alert.

"Yeah, no problem. Keep your eyes open. I've got a bad feeling about this. Something just doesn't feel right about this guy."

"I've got the same feeling. Nobody's leaving the hotel after dark and we've already locked things up here until morning."

"Great. I'm glad I've got somebody up there to keep an eye on things. Thanks, Eli."

"No problem. I'll wait to hear from you tomorrow, then."

"Talk at you then." Ben disconnected and Eli set his phone down as Danielle entered the room.

"Oh great. Having top secret spy talks with my brother again, Agent 007?" Danielle snapped at Eli.

"Nothing top secret. He just wanted me to know the guy was out of surgery but heavily sedated so he wasn't able to talk with him tonight. We plan to run in to the hospital tomorrow and ask some questions if he's awake and able to talk."

"Oh." Danielle sulked.

"Danielle, what do you want me to say?" He followed her to the bedroom and leaned against the open doorway, watching as she dropped herself down on the bed in a huff. Tiny had been sleeping on the bed, exhausted from too much Thanksgiving food, and lifted his heavy head at the intrusion, dropping it back on the mattress, snoring.

"I just need to process this."

"Why don't you get in bed and try to get some sleep. No sense worrying until we have the chance to talk to the guy, right?"

"I guess." She hid a yawn behind her hand and stretched her arms above her head. "But I want to come with you to the hospital tomorrow."

"We'll talk to your brother and see what he says."

****Chapter Seventeen****

Danielle was watching him, peeking around the corner of the hallway wall, but he tried his best to ignore her. Sending her to bed earlier and walking away had been one of the hardest things he'd ever had to do.

He wasn't sure he could do it again.

"Go to bed Danielle," he muttered without looking at her.

"I couldn't sleep." Pulling herself away from the wall, she gave up trying to hide and joined him in the living room. He closed his laptop and pushed back in his chair, making her jump back to get out of his way or be run over.

A good stiff drink was what he needed right now, but all he could find in her refrigerator was water and milk so he helped himself to a bottled water, refusing to look at her. He knew she'd be in her bedclothes, all satiny soft and barely concealing, he couldn't risk looking at her.

"Go to bed. Please."

He knew she wouldn't.

She had a stubborn streak the size of the universe.

"What are you writing?"

"Nothing you'd be interested in. Now go to bed. We have a busy day ahead of us tomorrow, we're going to need our sleep."

He had to put some distance between them so he kept walking, back into the living room and back to his computer, saving his file and shutting it down.

Tiny sat at the edge of the hallway watching them with only mild interest then finally dropped his weary body down to the carpet and closed his eyes.

Eli wished he could do the same.

"But I can't sleep. I thought I'd watch some television or something." She started toward the television, his hungry eyes following her across the room before he remembered to look away and head for his bed on the couch.

"You have a television in your bedroom, watch it in there. I'm going to hit the sack. It's late."

He rolled out his blankets and pillows on the couch, hoping she'd take the not-so-subtle hint.

Subtle was wasted on Danielle.

"You know, Roxanna isn't here. Why haven't you moved into the spare bedroom, it has to be more comfortable than the couch?"

Why wouldn't she just go to bed? He was barely keeping himself under control.

"No thanks. I can keep a better eye on things from out here. Now, go to bed. That's the last time I'm going to tell you." Thinking intimidation would work where patience hadn't, he was across the room in two long strides, invading her personal space, towering over her from behind.

"But...I can't..."

"You can't what?" he said close to her ear, his breath on her neck. She jumped when he spoke, obviously unaware he'd been standing so close, and spun around to face him. He picked her up by the armpits and pinned her to the wall with his body, chest to chest, hip to hip, thigh to thigh, trapping both of her hands above her head after sliding his hands up her arms in a slow, agonizing caress. When she dared to look into his eyes, he saw the dark heat of his own eyes reflected there, searing him from the inside out.

She opened her mouth to protest, or beg, he didn't know which, and he captured the sound with his lips as they crashed down to seal her fate, devouring her without mercy. At her whimper, he lowered his hands to her waist, releasing her hands to wrap around his neck as he lifted her, wrapping her legs around his hips, pulling away from the wall and carrying her down the hallway toward her bedroom. His kisses trailed down her quivering neck and under her chin, he could feel the purrs rumbling from her throat as his lips tasted her, and she held on tight.

Once in her bedroom, he carried them to the side of her bed and leaned over its surface, smoothing her arms and legs from around his body as he laid her gently on the mattress. Then, placing one last searing kiss on her drugged lips, he stepped back.

"Go to sleep, Danielle," he rasped, hearing his voice shake, then turned and walked out of the room.

She wouldn't be too happy with him right now, but he knew he was doing the right thing.

As he willed himself to make that trip down the hallway, away from her, toward the cold lonely couch, he heard something hit the door behind him. She cursed and slammed her bedroom door.

Tiny whimpered and hid behind Eli by the couch.

"Looks like you'll be spending the night with me, fella," he told the frightened puppy.

Eli was up and out of the apartment, sitting in front of

the hotel, by dawn the next morning, not looking forward to an early morning confrontation with his angry roommate. The cold steps at his backside were a stiff reminder of the warm bed he'd walked away from the night before.

Tiny was taking care of his business in his favorite spot in the nearby wooded area and hadn't returned yet when Eli heard the sound of cars approaching.

It was Ben, followed by one of his deputies in a separate car.

This was not good.

As they pulled in to park single file at the hotel turnaround, Eli walked out to meet them.

"Morning, Ben."

"Eli."

"Am I to assume that you come bearing bad news?"

"Unfortunately, yes. I got a call from the hospital a couple hours ago. Our guy, Wally Parker, walked out of the hospital sometime during the night and disappeared."

"Well, you've got to give the guy points for having the strength to stand upright from what I've heard of his injuries."

"That's not the half of it. You know the emergency room doctors who examined him and spoke of multiple bruises and recent trauma?" At Eli's nod, Ben continued.

"There was one injury, an old one, they failed to mention. An old scar, through-and-through on his left foot. They're pretty sure it was a bullet wound."

"Hmm, a bullet wound to one of his feet. Now why does that sound familiar?"

"Mitch Bromley was drummed out of the Guard after shooting himself in the foot. The left foot." Ben waited for Eli's reaction. "Damn it Eli! The bastard was right under our noses the whole time!"

"So, Wally Parker - the clumsy oaf who stabbed himself with a fork at our Thanksgiving table - and Mitch Bromley - the clumsy oaf who shot himself in the foot - are one and the same?"

"Hell of a deal, huh? Blood collected at the hospital will tell us for sure once we can run the DNA." Ben shook his head. "We need to get in his room, look through his stuff and see if we can get any clues as to where he could be hiding. Did he have a car? I came with search warrants for both."

"So, he hasn't gone back to his home over in…where did you say, somewhere on the other side of these woods?"

"Not yet. We're hoping he'll be stupid and walk right into our hands there. I've got a deputy there to watch for him."

"He has a car. It's parked over there, but I'll bet it's a rental."

"We still might find something. I'll have my deputy look it over while we check out his room. Is Danielle up and around?"

"Well, I don't know." Eli scratched his neck, not wanting to share too much with the other man. "She's not real happy with me right now so I'm out here. Not sure what mood she's going to be in."

Ben smirked and shook his head. "I don't even want to know what you did now." As a deputy approached them, Ben pointed out the car in question and asked him to check it out.

"Are you sure, Sheriff?" the deputy asked after getting a good look at the car.

"Yeah, why?"

"Well, I've seen this car before. When we were up here investigating that shooting. I drove by a guy, he'd pulled over and said he was just finishing up on changing a flat tire. That wouldn't have been suspicious but when I looked in the trunk, the spare was still in there. I thought something was funny about it at the time, but I was in a hurry to get here so I just let him go."

"Really, now that's interesting. Why don't we pop the

trunk on this baby and see what he was hiding in there."
The deputy reached in the driver's side of the unlocked car
to pull the trunk release, watching in silence as the trunk
popped open. Ben pulled on a pair of gloves then reached
inside, lifting the spare cover and tossing it on the ground
behind them then unscrewed the bolt holding the small do-
nut spare tire resting there. He tossed the bolts aside as they
came loose and lifted the tire aside.

"Well, well, well...what do we have here, gentle-
men?" Ben lifted the gun for a closer look.

"I'd say it looks like a nine millimeter, Sheriff. I'm
guessing that it's missing a few bullets, right?" Eli felt the
pieces coming together. "We've finally caught a break. I'd
also say we really need to catch this guy, though I am com-
forted to know he no longer has a gun in his possession...that we know of."

"This is definitely a step in the right direction!" Ben
beamed.

"What is that?" Danielle snapped as she walked up on
them. "And where did you find it? Whose car is that?"

"It belongs to our guest, Wally Parker. It would seem
that he's not a nice fellow after all."

"Shut up, Eli. Are you okay, Danielle? You don't look
so good." Ben watched as Danielle sprinted back inside the

hotel. "Here, Deputy, will you please handle this for a minute, I want to check on Danni."

As Ben went after his sister, Tiny came crashing out of the woods. In his mouth was, again, another personal treasure. This time, though, there was something about his find that had Eli looking a little closer.

He followed Tiny to where he usually stashed his treasures, behind the rose bushes. What he found there had him shouting for the deputy and running inside to get Ben.

"Ben, I think you need to get out here!" he shouted then ran back outside to keep an eye on what he'd found.

Ben joined him and the deputy as they knelt in the rose gardens, poking their find with a stick.

"What now?" Ben asked as he skidded to a halt beside Eli.

"Do these look like human bones to you?"

"Those over there, I don't know, but that one…that is definitely a human hand! Jesus! What the hell is going on around here? Where did these come from?"

"Tiny has been dragging them here, one by one, from somewhere in the woods," Eli replied, shaken at what they'd found.

"This is not good. This is not good at all."

****Chapter Eighteen****

"Okay, Ruth, Edna. What have you and Vic been up to, and don't deny it, I know Vic had something to do with that man being stabbed. He hasn't made an appearance around here since and now they've found a gun in the man's car. For all we know he's a murderer! A killer! He's been living here under our roof all this time!" Danielle paced as the Manchester sisters stood watching helplessly.

"Calm down, sweetie. It won't do any good for you to make yourself sick worrying over this. Vic took care of that evil, evil man and now he's gone. Everything is okay now, everything is fine." Ruth tried to reassure her.

"No! Everything is definitely not okay, Ruth! Everything is not fine! Don't you see?" Danielle felt she was nearing hysteria. "What's going to happen now? I need to be sure my guests are all going to be safe here...I need to…I need…I don't know what I need!" She dropped her shaky body on the couch and leaned forward with her elbows on her knees, holding her head in her hands.

"Danni!" Roxanna crashed through the door and rushed to Danielle to envelope her in a hug on the couch. "I came as soon as Ben called. Are you okay?"

"I'm fine, Roxie. I'm so glad you're here. I was so scared not knowing where you were. There's a maniac out there."

"Yeah. Ben told me. It's freaking awesome! There's *tons* of cop cars out there."

"Yeah, I know. The guy was staying here all along! Right under my roof!"

"We've tried to tell her we've been keeping an eye on him," Edna interrupted.

"What do you mean? Why would you keep an eye on him? Did you know something about the guy before now?" Danielle asked them, but they wouldn't meet her eye. "Ruth? Edna? What do you know?"

"Well, we didn't know anything. Not until the other day when he tried to push you down the stairs…again. Then we knew for sure he was up to something."

"He what?" Danielle screeched and jumped to her feet to face the two ghosts. "When was this?"

"What…the first time? Or the second time?"

"He tried to push me down the stairs twice?"

"Well, the first time we just thought he was clumsy or something. It was right after he moved in. We thought he'd tripped when he came so close to pushing you down the stairs, but he missed and fell down the staircase himself…well, kind of after we pushed him a little. It was a terrible fall, actually. We don't know how he survived that one," Ruth commented reasonably. "Then, when was the second time, sister? Two days ago?"

"Yes dear. Wait, no. Two days before your dinner celebration. Yes, that was it. That's when he did it again." Edna nodded.

"Thank you, dear. Yes, it was a couple of days before your dinner. You were vacuuming again. He came out of his room and lunged at you. He is quite an evil man, I must say."

"So how did I not see this?" Danielle asked, amazed she could have been that close to disaster without even knowing it.

"That vacuum cleaner always was a loud one, you probably couldn't hear anything." Ruth looked at her sister for confirmation, who nodded.

"Why did he miss that time?"

"Oh, my. It was Vic. He was so masterful, you would have been proud. He simply picked up the man and threw him against the wall away from you. He saved your life. Quite possibly. Oh, dear. It's most distressing to think about what would have happened if Vic hadn't been there." She fanned her face dramatically and Edna hugged her close.

As Danielle digested the information, she dropped her head to her chest in concentration and stood with her hands on her hips taking deep breaths. When she finally looked up, it was rage, not fear, consuming her.

"Oh dear. Are you mad at us, honey?" Ruth asked.

"No, Ruth, of course not. You've been protecting me. But I'm through living in fear. This guy is not going to get the best of me. How dare he! Threatening my hotel, your hotel. The weasel." She stormed out of her apartment looking for her brother. Ruth and Edna disappeared as she walked through them. Roxanna followed close behind.

"BEN!" Danielle yelled as she walked through the lobby and spotted her brother through the front windows standing with Eli in the rose gardens. Bursting through the front door with the plan to confront her brother, her steps slowed as Ben stood and walked toward her with his hands up to stop her progress.

"Stop, Danielle. Stay right there. We have a crime scene that we need to preserve, some new evidence, and you need to stay back."

"What new evidence? I already know about the gun. Are all these cops around here just because you found that gun? Wait a minute. Those aren't your men, what's with all these cops? What's going on here? Ben? What have you found?" Danielle tried to look over his shoulder at where Eli was kneeling, but Ben pushed her back.

"Will you, please, just do as I tell you and stay inside where you'll be safe?"

"Why? Ben? Why am I not safe?" Danielle pressed him.

"Because the guy walked out of the hospital in the middle of the night and we don't know where he is." Ben told her. "So, I need to you to stay inside until we can check the area and set up a perimeter. Will you, please, do that for me?"

"Oh, okay. Can we take Tiny with us?" she asked in a small voice and Roxanna grabbed her hand for support.

"Of course. Tiny!" He called to the dog that had been sitting obediently near the rose gardens watching Eli. "Tiny, come!" Tiny leaped from his crouch and loped over to Danielle.

"Now, please go inside and wait until you hear from us. Oh, and get the keys to Wally Parker's room, leave them on the front desk so we can take a look around. Thanks." Ben walked away from her.

She wanted to ask more questions but she caught Eli watching her.

His eyes locked with hers for a moment then he looked away to speak to Ben as he approached him.

He and her brother were in full cop mode.

So he wasn't thinking clearly when he'd rolled out of that hospital bed and snuck out. He only knew that he needed to get as far away from there as possible. With no clothes, he had to grab a shirt, pants, and shoes from another patient on his way out and was wearing the over-sized garments now.

His hand was heavily bandaged and hurt like crazy but the cold temperatures outside actually seemed to help by keeping him numb. Whatever drugs they'd given him made his brain foggy, slowing him down when he'd stumbled out of the hospital in the middle of the night.

The goal was to get to his home, get some warmer clothing and supplies for trekking in the woods, and try to get some transportation. The hospital they'd taken him to was only a few blocks from his house so he'd finally caught a break.

When he'd reached his house that night, there were police cars parked in front and around the block. They were unmarked cars, but...what...did they think he was stupid? He knew unmarked police cars when he saw them.

Cutting across his neighbor's back yard, out of sight, he made it to his back door, letting himself in with the key he always stashed over the door.

He was careful not to turn on any lights and dragged himself to the back bedroom to drop his exhausted body on the mattress.

He woke early the next morning, peeking out the window to make sure none of the cops had discovered him. Dressed in warmer clothes, he gathered up the necessary supplies for his journey, shoveled down some food and bundled himself into his parka, slipping out the back door undetected. He was able to squeeze his trim body between the hedge and fence to get from the back yard to the front. When he hit the sidewalk he walked, cool as you please, right by the undercover cops parked at the curb and disappeared around the block.

He would really have preferred to have some transportation, but since there was no way he would have been

able to pull his car out of the driveway without being de-
tected, he had to walk. The hotel was only on the other side
of the woods so he knew what trees would shelter him if he
needed to spend the night there and which paths to take
when he'd need to hide.

The game was on and nearing an end.

He didn't have the strength to go all Rambo on any-
body but he did have adrenaline pumping him to finish the
job at hand.

He needed to get that girl.

She and that miserable hotel and all of its spooky in-
habitants had ruined his life and it was time he made her
pay!

Tucking his injured hand in his coat pocket, he
stepped off the sidewalk, trudging up the hill leading him
into the woods.

****Chapter Nineteen****

"We have the cadaver dogs working the wooded area Danielle pinpointed with her pictures. They haven't found anything yet but we know they will," Ben told Eli as they waited by the front steps of the hotel. It was an unseasonably warm November day for Iowa so they didn't have snow or freezing temperatures to deal with or to compromise any evidence.

It had been several hours since they'd found the bones in the rose garden and the air crackled with frustrated tension. The search of Wally's room had cemented their suspicions about the guy when they'd found torn clothing matching a scrap of fabric left behind in Danielle's apartment at the time of the break in.

They were waiting for a their big break in the case, news that the manhunt in the area looking for Mitch Brom-

215

ley - a.k.a. Wally Parker - had found the guy. Eli worried that Bromley would still find a way to get past their patrols, he knew he wasn't going to give up until he'd gotten to Danielle. The psychology of a psychopath told him they didn't just give up or quit until they'd reached their goal or died trying. Ben had whatever manpower he could spare patrolling the area day and night.

It was only a matter of time.

He had a feeling Bromley was coming back to the hotel - was possibly already here watching them - and they needed to be ready.

"We'll get the guy. I'm not going to let anyone hurt my sister." Eli sensed the determination in Ben's voice. This man would give his life to protect his sister...if it came to that. "He's clumsy, he'll make a mistake and we'll be there. If he's living in the woods, the winter weather alone will flush him out eventually."

"Yeah."

"Danielle's not a happy camper. By the time Bromley surfaces, she may be ready to skin him alive with her bare hands and I'd let her," Ben said and Eli agreed, all too aware of her temper.

"Roxie can handle her," Eli said. "One of these days somebody's going to let me in on the secret between those two. There's something strange about this place and I just can't put my finger on it."

"You don't know the half of it," Ben said, then turned away when one of his men shouted at him from the edge of the woods. "Maybe they've found something. Come on."

He'd been living in the tool shed behind the hotel waiting for his chance. The place was crawling with cops, small town good-old-boys all hot to catch him.

He wasn't really big on getting caught so he was hanging out in the cozy insulated tool shed munching on his trail mix bars and water from his stash.

They had no clue, again, that he was living right under their very noses.

As he was mentally patting himself on the back for his cleverness, he heard voices from the front of the hotel and then footsteps as several people ran past the shed.

Could he have just scored his one chance?

He peeked out the front door of the shed.

Sure enough, the cops who had been patrolling the area behind the hotel were all gone. He crept out of the shed, to the corner of the hotel to see what was going on in front. They gathered at the edge of the woods then disappeared into the screen of trees. Every one of them!

The coast was clear.

This was his chance!

Keeping his body close to the wall of the building, he inched his way to the front door, watching over his shoulder in case the cops returned.

They didn't.

He reached the front door with no problem and let himself in. The front lobby was deserted but he could hear somebody rattling away at a computer in the office so he had to hurry to the back apartment, the one he knew belonged to her.

As he reached the door, he grasped the doorknob with his uninjured hand.

He couldn't believe the door was unlocked!

It was a little awkward with his bandaged hand stuffed uselessly in his pocket, but his blood was pumping so hard in his ears, the adrenaline coursing through his veins that he couldn't have stopped now for anything.

He pushed the door open with the shoulder of his bad hand.

He was greeted with silence when he entered the room.

It was empty.

Was she out in the hotel somewhere and he just didn't

see her?

Had he missed her?

Then he heard her voice in the bedroom. She was coming down the hallway, talking to somebody.

He had to move now!

He rushed to the kitchen to hide against the wall where he could grab her as she entered from the hallway. Looking around for a weapon, he cursed himself for being in such a hurry to leave the shed that he'd forgotten to bring something.

Sitting on the counter behind him was a knife block.

He yanked out the first handle he could reach without looking at it and brandished it in front of him, waiting for her to appear from around the hall.

She was still talking to somebody but he couldn't worry about who the other person was, he'd worry about the other person later.

He could feel her breathing.

Smell her skin.

She was close.

His fingers tingled, imagining what she would feel like when he finally got his hands on her.

She was real close...

Then, there she was!

She cleared the wall, her back partially turned so she didn't see him. He leaped out from his hiding place, reaching for her, the handle of his weapon outstretched.

Instead of feeling himself leaping forward, he found himself thrust backward and hitting the refrigerator, the long vertical door handle hitting him in the middle of his back. He dropped the knife and must have screamed for she turned to face him.

It wasn't fear on her face.

She was laughing!

She was laughing at him!

He pulled himself away from the door to advance on her and that's when the huge beast came out of nowhere.

The last thing he remembered before passing out was the feeling of being run over by a truck, unable to breathe.

"Seriously, he was going to attack me with a butter knife! A butter knife! He's an embarrassment as a criminal. He gives all criminals a bad name!" Danielle was ranting as Ben watched a handcuffed and unconscious Mitch Bromley being hauled out of her apartment on a stretcher. He let his sister vent, she had it coming. "...miserable excuse for a killer if you ask me..." she mumbled, stalking back and forth the length of her apartment while Tiny followed every step. "And who's my big hero? You are, Tiny! You are so brave, knocking him down and sitting on him like that. My big brave puppy, yes you are."

Danielle dropped to her knees to give Tiny hugs and kisses and he gave her a whole body tail wag, slobbering all over her as Ben watched.

"Any kisses for us? After all the work we've done out there?" Eli asked from the doorway and received a scowl from Danielle.

"Where were you when he just walked right into my apartment?" she asked.

"Don't worry, none of the men who abandoned their posts were any of mine. I have a feeling their superiors are none too pleased with them right now either." Ben could finally breathe a sigh of relief that the guy was caught, he just wasn't happy with how it happened.

"Yeah. When Tiny had him down I really wanted to give the guy a few kicks, but seriously, he was such a miserable wreck I almost felt sorry for him!"

"Don't feel too sorry for the guy. They're still digging up the bodies out there. He may have been clumsy and ineffective in getting you, but his other victims weren't so lucky. It's going to be weeks, months even, before we'll be able to identify them," Ben said. "Now, I think I'd like to get my boy back home."

"Who, Tiny?" Danielle asked, pausing to wipe doggie drool off her face. "Oh, but I'm going to miss my baby so much. It was nice having him here. Thanks, Ben." She pouted.

"You were probably about out of dog food anyway." Ben turned to leave, Tiny at his side. "I'm going to go check on things outside, it's getting dark out and they're probably ready to call it a day."

"Well, I guess I can get my things and move them back to my room. You won't be needing me here any-more." Eli rolled up the few clothes he had on the couch, slung his laptop under his arm and headed for the door.

Danielle wanted to say something to make him stay but knew it would be best if he left. It wasn't like he was walking out of her life or anything, he would still be in his apartment upstairs, for now.

"So, what are you going to do now?" she asked, as he passed her on the way to the door, unable to stop herself.

"Now? Well, I return to my room, where I had origi-nally planned to write my book. I get my book done then I head back to the city. Why?"

Heading back to the city?

"No reason, just wondering. Well, I guess you'd better get to it then."

"Look, Danielle. You're just feeling a little bit of a crash from the adrenaline you've been running on. It's perfectly normal. Give yourself some time. Relax. You'll get back to your normal routine soon enough. Trust me." He turned and left her apartment, the closing of the door shutting her down as effectively as though he'd said his final goodbye.

Trust me, he says.

Things were never going to get back to normal. Danielle wasn't even sure she knew what normal was anymore.

****Chapter Twenty****

Eli couldn't sleep so he did what he normally did as a cop trying to shake off the day's work, he left his apartment to take a walk. He would have walked outside but the hotel had been locked up for the night and he didn't want to wake anyone.

As he reached the foot of the staircase, he heard voices coming from the front lobby and realized it was Danielle. She was sitting in one of the lobby chairs with a book and talking to herself again. As he walked across the room toward her, she stopped talking and watched his approach.

"It's after eleven o'clock, what are you doing up?" She visibly tensed as he got near.

"Couldn't sleep, a holdover from my days as a cop, I've always had trouble sleeping after a case wrapped up. What's your excuse?" he asked, standing in front of her as she unfolded herself and rose from her chair.

"Same, can't sleep. I come out here to unwind. It makes me feel closer to, well, some people who used to live here. I was just going to make myself a cup of cocoa. Would you like some?"

"Yeah, sure. Why not."

If he were smart, he would have said no and returned to his room, putting as much distance between him and this woman as possible.

He wasn't feeling particularly smart tonight.

Danielle tucked the book under her arm and led him to her apartment, nervous to be alone with him again, but she knew when she'd been sitting in the lobby that she'd hoped he would appear, that he would hear her silent appeal for him to come to her, down that staircase, and share the quiet darkness of the hotel with her.

Her apartment was too quiet since he'd moved out.

Reaching her unlocked apartment, she took a couple of steps inside and turned on the lights, leaning down to set her book on a table.

The door clicked shut behind her.

His arms wrapped around her, pulling her back into him as he backed up against the door. A sigh escaped her and she relaxed into his arms, leaning her head back on his shoulder and his lips were instantly on the flesh of her neck.

"Eli, this isn't a good idea," she whispered but her body melted against his. Nowhere in her mind or body was she registering the word no.

"This is the best idea I've had in a long time." His lips continued their torturing path at the side of her neck, his tongue teasing behind one ear. She turned her head, her lips searching for his and he turned her to face him, his hands on a slow journey down her body, to her hips to pull her snugly into him, his lips never losing contact with the flesh of her neck.

"...but, I don't even like you..." she mumbled.

"...sure you do..."

"...you're bossy...controlling..." His mouth closed over hers, his tongue persuading her lips open so he could slip inside for a long drugging kiss.

The room faded into the background, her senses so focused on his kiss, she barely registered him swinging her up into his arms. He stalked down the hallway to her bedroom where he lowered her to the floor next to the bed, letting her body slide slowly down his before setting her feet on the floor.

Pushing her shirt up and over her head, he tossed it away. Then his shirt joined hers on the floor and he pulled her to him, the touch of his chest against hers bringing her ecstasy and pain, forcing a moan from her lips. The sound seemed to set him on fire. She was picked up and dropped on the bed with Eli on top, settling his body into the cradle of her hips as his mouth crashed down on hers.

Everything was happening so fast, but not fast enough. She couldn't get enough of him, wanted to wrap herself around him until she'd felt and tasted every inch of his hot, pulsing, tightly muscled flesh.

Her fingers ran through his hair, holding his face to hers as they feasted on each other with abandon, her legs gripping him, settling him deeper into her core, a liquid heat burning at her chest and flowing to where their bodies were only separated by thin layers of clothing.

She felt his hands roam greedily over her body then cup her breasts and his mouth left hers to blaze a path to one hard nipple, suckling the nub as her body bucked under him, begging for more.

And he gave more, licking his way to the other nipple while his hands traveled down to slip under the elastic of her pajama bottoms and panties, smoothing them down her hips, thighs, and feet...off her body, leaving her exposed for him to explore. He stretched out beside her on the bed and his hand caressed over her bared skin, up her leg from ankle to her thighs, upward, over her trembling belly, back across her breasts and to her neck where he slid it around to cup her neck, holding her head steady as he dropped a searing kiss on her open lips.

Through curious but hungry eyes, she watched as he pulled away to remove the rest of his clothing, palming a couple of packets from one of the pockets and setting them on the mattress beside them. Then he was back, covering her body with his, pressing her into the mattress with his skin to hers, molding their hot, damp bodies together, resting between her open thighs but otherwise not moving. Supporting his upper body on his elbows at either side of her head, he paused to study her face then lowered his mouth to tease her lips with his, licking, tasting, savoring.

She couldn't wait anymore, she rose up to meet him, wrapping her arms around his back and only then did he start to move, sliding one hand down the side of her body, lifting one of her thighs, his hand whispered across her hip toward the center of her heat, entering her damp core. She called out his name, begging him to stop, begging for more.

"Yes, Danielle? Tell me what you want," he whispered against her neck.

"…nnnno…"

"What do you want? Tell me." She knew he was watching her face, could feel the heat of his dark eyes on hers as his wicked fingers thrust in and out of her body. "Danielle. Open your eyes. Look at me," he commanded quietly, his hand stopped its torture. She heard him ripping open the foil package as he sheathed himself and her eyes opened, focusing on his.

"You…yessss," she hissed, "…you…"

And she realized it was true.

His mouth captured hers as his body plunged deeply into hers. She wrapped her legs around him and his growl rumbled through her, a thunderstorm sending lightning bolts of sensation through her body.

Eli lay on his back, still in Danielle's bed, as she slept beside him.

He hadn't planned this, but he knew it had been inevitable. What he hadn't known was how earth shattering it would be, they'd made love twice and he still wanted more. He'd thought after one night, he'd be able to walk away and return to his life in Chicago and not look back. But here he was lying in her bed wondering how he was going to walk away from her. When her life had been in danger, he hadn't trusted anyone but himself to keep her safe. He'd never intended for his stay at the hotel to be anything more than a short retreat to get him past his writer's block and get his book done, but instead he was thinking of waking every morning with this aggravating woman. Just thinking of her was making his body grow hard again.

Turning his head to look at her as she slept, she looked so sweet and innocent, no hint of the sassy girl he'd grown to know and...what?

Love?

No...not possible.

Was it?

She moaned in her sleep and he rolled toward her, spooning her from behind. In sleep, her body wiggled into him and his body hardened painfully in response. He tightened his arm around her and pulled her up close so his head rested beside hers on the pillow.

Yeah, probably just lust.

He couldn't possibly be in love.

Slow, burning kisses covered the back of her neck and she stretched into them. A hard male body molded to hers and bare skin slid across damp bare skin, one arm wrapping around her to caress her breast. She moaned and arched her back, pressing into the hardness at her back. The hand that had been caressing her breast, aroused them both to hard peaks then traveled down the front of her body to bury hot fingers in the dampness between her thighs, pulling her tightly back against the hard shaft. Shock waves trembled through her body, her fuzzy brain still on the edges of sleep, and she moved as if in a dream.

As she rolled slightly onto her pillow, hugging it to her chest, she pulled one leg up, pressing into the hand she imagined caressing her there, on the edge of ecstasy, her entire body inflamed and aroused. In the fuzzy background of her brain, she felt him roll her over, settle between her thighs and drive into her, holding her still for his possession, driving her over the edge.

She woke from the depths of her sensual dream, riding the wave of her orgasm as he pulled out then thrust into her repeatedly then went still, growling her name.

"Good morning, Rox!" Roxanna was catching up on some light housekeeping in the front lobby when Danielle came waltzing out of her apartment, a little too cheerful for early morning hours.

"Yeah, whatever." Roxanna mumbled.

"So what's going on around here today? Anyone else

up and around yet?"

"Nope. Same old, same old."

"Nobody?"

"Nope." Roxanna didn't know who Danielle was in-terested in hearing about, but decided it was best not to ask. She wasn't sure she even wanted to know.

"Oh, well I thought we should be getting the Christ-mas decorations out and working on that. What do you think?"

"Yeah, whatever." *Goth did not do Christmas*, Roxan-na mumbled to herself, but doubted Danielle was listening.

"Try not to get so excited my Goth friend."

"Bite me."

"Great. I'll start hauling the stuff up from the base-ment then."

"Oh, by the way," Roxanna said. "Eli will be leaving tomorrow. He says he finished what he needed to do while he was here and is ready to head back home before winter hits."

"What did you say?"

"I said, Eli is leaving tomorrow. Didn't he say any-thing to you about that?"

"No, he didn't."

"Oh, well. You two never did seem to get along very

well, you probably scared him away." Roxanna smirked to herself but kept dusting.

"I chased him away didn't I...?"

"What? Of course not. I was just kidding. For all I know you two are madly in love, something sick like that, but what do I know?" When she heard nothing from Danielle, she turned, gasping at what she saw there. "God, Danielle. What did you do, fall in love with the guy?"

"Of course not. I don't know, what do I know about such a thing? No, of course not." Danielle turned away.

Roxanna grabbed her arm and spun her around to face her. "You know our rule. We don't get involved with the guests, ever. Did you go and fall for the guy?" Roxanna gripped her by both arms and shook her to get an answer.

"It's a little more than that."

"You slept with him?" Roxanna shrieked.

"Shh!" They stared at each other in silence then Roxanna clucked her tongue and returned to her work.

"So, Little Miss Too-tough-to-ever-fall-for-some-dumb-guy, Jacobs."

"It's not funny."

"No, it's not. Get over it. He's leaving." Footsteps sounded on the stairs, silencing the rest of their conversation.

"Good morning, ladies!" Eli greeted them then wiped the smile off his face when Danielle shot daggers at him and stalked away toward the basement.

"What's the matter with her?" he asked, taking a tentative step in her direction.

"Nothing, and, no you really don't want to be going after her right now. Trust me."

"I need to run to town, I should be gone a couple of hours," he said, watching Danielle's retreating back. "I think, maybe I need to talk to Danielle."

"Seriously, dude. No," Roxanna said.

"Okay, maybe you're right. Catch you later." Tossing his keys from hand to hand, he walked out the front door.

"Are all men clueless?" Roxanna muttered to Sebastian, who had appeared as Eli was leaving.

Danielle stomped up from the basement carrying the first stack of Christmas decorations.

"You know what? I really need to get some yard work done, finish up on the rose gardens. Is it okay if I bail on you and the Christmas decorations for now?" Danielle asked, dropping the box in front of the plate glass lobby windows.

"Knock yourself out." Roxanna waved her away. "But don't expect me to like it if you make me decorate this place. Christmas...PFFT! Maybe if we had a black Christmas tree ...*THAT* I would like to see."

****Chapter Twenty-One****

Again, he'd outsmarted those stupid cops. They'd hauled him to the hospital and tried to lock him up in the mental ward, but he lucked out and got some new guy checking him in at the desk and he was able to slip away when the guy wasn't paying attention. The cops who were supposed to be guarding him were flirting with some nurses down the hall.

He just walked right out of the hospital and hopped in a parked car!

These small town hicks and their trusting ways!

The driver had left the keys in the ignition.

It was like destiny was begging him to steal it! And here he was, driving up the hill to the hotel again with nobody to stop him. He had a close call there when that guy in the red Mustang passed him on the road about an hour ago but the guy didn't stop or even look at him in passing.

Parking his stolen car along the side of the road so nobody at the hotel would hear him drive up, he walked the rest of the way, functioning on pure adrenaline now, he couldn't sleep, couldn't eat, he just kept going like that damned Energizer Bunny.

The woman had to die and if he had to destroy the hotel and everybody in it - including himself - all the better.

As he neared the hotel he saw her.

She was in front of the hotel wrapping burlap around something…bushes maybe.

There was a rake leaning on the wall nearby, would that be his weapon?

No.

He needed something bigger and more lethal.

Then he saw what he thought looked like a gas can sitting on the ground in front of the tool shed and inspiration struck.

That's it!

He sprang into action, grabbing the filled-to-the-brim can in his good hand and sprinting to the front doors of the hotel, crashing through the doors and into the hotel lobby.

Danielle stood, stretching her tired back.

The last thing she needed to do before finishing up in the garden was to give the bushes one good watering before the first frost.

Taking a step toward the tool shed, she was almost knocked off her feet as a figure dashed in front of her and ran inside the hotel.

Something looked familiar about the heavily cloaked, hunched over, limping individual.

Then it hit her.

It was that crazy Wally Parker - Mitch Bromley - whatever his name was.

Damn it!

She needed to have a serious talk with her brother about the poor job his men did in keeping a prisoner in custody!

She was already in a piss poor mood, and the yard work hadn't taken the edge off her mood. Now that stupid fool was back.

This was the last straw!

She marched to the front doors, fire burning in her eyes and fury running through her blood. With both hands on the double doors of the hotel, she burst into the lobby and came to a stop, facing the man standing in the middle of the floor, dousing himself with the contents of the can.

"You're all dead! Do you hear me! You've messed with the wrong guy and now you are all going to die!" he screamed, emptying the can over his head and tossing it away from him. Then he started patting his pockets, looking for something. He stopped, panicking as he looked Danielle straight in the eye where she stood not three feet in front of him.

"Looking for something?" Danielle taunted with a snarl. "Some matches, maybe? Roxie, give the guy a pack of matches. Let's watch him burn." At Roxanna's questioning look, Danielle nodded, silently asking her to trust her. Roxanna tossed a pack from behind the counter. They bounced off the man and fell to the floor. She leaned on the counter, calmly petting Sebastian while they both watched the man.

"You crazy bitch! I'm going to burn the place down!" he shrieked and reached for the matches, picking them up from the floor but not lighting them. "What's the matter with you people! I'm going to light myself on fire and burn this place down!"

"Knock yourself out, asshole." Danielle was deceptively calm as she stood watching and waiting.

"Son-of-a-bitch! You're even crazier than I am!" He made a move toward Danielle but she'd had enough.

Danielle lunged at him and knocked him back against the counter, punching him in the face and watching as he crumpled to the floor. Dropping on top of him, she continued hitting him, taking out all of her frustrations out on the already battered man.

"What's the matter, big man?" She hit one side of his face. "Get up and fight like a man, you coward!" She hit the other side. "Are you going to let a woman beat you, low life?" She was pummeling him even after he'd passed out and would have kept going if somebody hadn't lifted her, kicking and punching, off his prone body. She felt the band of steel around her waist but managed to get one last kick to the guy's body before she was pulled away from him.

"Calm down, Danielle. He's unconscious, he's not going to hurt you. You can stop now," Eli whispered close to her ear, holding her tight against him until she calmed down. As her breathing returned to normal, Eli loosened his hold but didn't release her.

"Are you okay?" He turned her to face him, holding her by both arms.

"Let. Me. Go." She ground out through painfully clenched teeth and he released her, holding his hands up in surrender. "I have work to do outside." She picked up the watering can and stalked out the front doors, bumping into her brother as he was coming in, not stopping to acknowledge him in any way.

"Sis?" When she didn't respond, Ben turned to Eli for answers, who shook his head at the law man. Then he saw the bloody, unconscious man on the floor. "Does somebody want to tell me what's going on around here?"

"That sister of yours has a little bit of a temper on her." Eli knelt beside the man, checking for a pulse in the man's bruised neck.

"Is this her handiwork?" Ben slapped handcuffs on the man on the floor, then stood, not too concerned that the man would get away from him any time soon.

"She beat the living daylights out of the poor guy. Something tells me that doesn't surprise you."

Ben shook his head, looking down at the damaged body on the floor then smiling at Eli.

"This has been coming for over ten years. I hope she got it out of her system otherwise it's not a good idea to be around her right now."

"So, how did you get here so fast? I just got back from town myself when I happened upon this."

"They called me from the hospital when they realized he'd escaped again. It was obvious where he would go."

"Yeah. There's not an inch of his body that isn't broken, battered, or bruised yet he still keeps coming back for more. How does he keep going?"

"The true nature of a psychopath, I suppose. They seem to be able to block out pain. But trust me, this time I'm taking him in for myself. He's not getting away again. By the way, I was just watching the excavation of the bodies in the woods. We should be wrapping that up in a couple of days. Looks like we have at least seven bodies accounted for, seven graves."

"Good luck identifying them."

"Yeah," Ben said then noticed the body on the floor move as though he was coming around. "Look, I'd better get this guy in my car and back where he belongs."

Eli helped Ben lift his prisoner to his feet then followed him outside as he locked the man in the back seat of his car.

****Chapter Twenty-Two****

"So, great! I can meet you tomorrow with my manuscript." Eli spoke with his agent as he paced his room, his cell phone glued to his ear. The sooner he got his book delivered to his agent the better.

"Yeah, I'm here." His agent was talking to him while he'd been spacing off. "Lunch? Yeah, name the place and I'll be there. How about I call you when I get into town, okay? Talk to you then."

His few bags were packed and waiting for him by the door so he grabbed them and let himself out of the cozy room he'd called home for the better part of two months.

The descent down the grand staircase seemed like the longest walk of his life. For the first time since his short stay in the old hotel he heard the creaking of each step, the smooth polish of the perfectly maintained banister flowing beneath his hand, and the light static spark as the soles of his shoes rubbed against the carpeted treads. Roxanna was waiting for him behind the front desk, her dark eyes watching him approach. Setting his things down beside the counter, he stepped up to the desk and forced a smile.

"So, you're really leaving us."

"Yeah, you sure do know how to show a guy a good time. This hotel has been like a roller coaster ride."

"Never a dull moment," she smirked.

"Danielle in her apartment?" He knew the answer but still felt compelled to ask, stalling.

"Yeah."

"Does she know I'm leaving?"

"Yeah." Eli digested the information then nodded. There wouldn't be a hug or kiss goodbye.

"Well, I guess this is it. You tell her goodbye for me?"

"Sure."

He handed her his credit card, signed off on the receipt she handed him, then picked up his bags, pocketing the card and receipt.

"Eli?"

"Yeah, Roxie?"

"She's just stubborn sometimes, she's had a rough life...some really bad stuff..."

"Don't worry, I'm not afraid of Danielle. I just need to get back to Chicago and take care of some business. You take it easy, Rox."

"Yeah. Bye, Eli."

The ache in her arms and shoulders was bone deep, searing a path down her body, punishing her for not taking a break, but still she couldn't stop. She had to keep scrubbing, disinfecting, sterilizing every surface. If she didn't she would still smell him there, the pain in her back was nothing compared to the pain she felt when she caught his scent. There was nothing she could do to control her body's reaction to the musky scent of him, it was everywhere in the room. If the bedcovers weren't so strong with his scent, she would have dropped her weary body on top of it a long time ago, just for a much-needed nap.

No, she couldn't stop.

Danielle had been cleaning the room for two days and it just wasn't working for her. Through the strong ammonia smell of the bleach she'd used to scrub the floors, she could still detect the fragrance, the essence that was Eli. The only thing left to do was to strip the bedclothes, again, and wash them...with bleach this time. She didn't care if the colors ran or it weakened the fabric of the old quilts, she had to bleach them. It was the only way.

With stomach growling at her, protesting the lack of food she'd been giving it lately, she grabbed the corners of the bedcovers and rolled them off the bed, bundling them in the center of the bed before hauling them out of the room.

Ben dropped in at the hotel later that morning and after a quick stop at the front desk, went to Danielle's apartment to check on her, knocking on the door and letting himself in.

"Danielle? Are you here?" He went looking for her in the bedroom. She'd just come out of the shower and was clad in her baggy bathrobe, towel drying her hair.

"Ben? What are you doing here in the middle of the day?"

"I just wanted to make sure you were okay. You look a little on the pale side. Roxie says you've been a drag." He'd never seen his sister sick, never known her to let her guard down or show weakness so he grew concerned at the dark circles under her eyes and pale complexion where he'd normally see a tanned and healthy face.

"She doesn't know what she's talking about. I'm fine."

"Still, I have to agree with Rox. You aren't looking so

good. Haven't you been eating?" Ben studied his sister more closely, noticing her shaky hands as she handled the towel.

"Oh, stop it. You two are a couple of worry-warts."

"You're obviously not fine, sis. You've lost weight, you're pale, and look at your hands shaking. When was the last time you ate a decent meal?" Ben scanned her face for clues. "You aren't taking care of yourself, I can tell by looking at you."

"I've just been busy getting ready for the Holidays. I have lots to do." She defended herself but he wasn't buying it.

"Yeah, whatever," he said then changed the subject. "Well, I have an early Christmas present for you. I left it out front with Roxie. Do you want me to bring it in?"

"I love presents! Yes, bring it in!" She tried to follow but he held her back.

"I'll be right back." He turned to leave the room after pushing her to sit on the bed and wait.

A commotion from the hallway and a loud scratching noise, then the thundering sound of big doggie paws announced the arrival of Tiny a split second before he came crashing into her room to land on top of her on the bed, covering her face in excited doggie slobber. When she heard a scuffling sound beside the bed, she leaned over to investigate. What she found was a wiggling, squirming, whining miniature version of Tiny trying - and failing - to jump up on the bed.

She looked up to find Ben leaning in the doorway of her bedroom with Roxanna.

"What is this?" she asked.

"Well, the big dog on the bed is Tiny. I think you've already met. And the smaller version on the floor is your Christmas present, you'll have to name him for yourself."

"You got me a puppy? Honest? You got me a puppy?"

"Isn't he just the cutest, ugliest little thing you've ever seen?" Roxanna said as she watched Danielle scratch, pet and coo over the puppy.

"I brought a supply of puppy food, it's in the office for now. It'll get you through a couple of months, hopefully. You're on your own after that. He and Tiny are brothers - distant brothers - but with the same sire and bitch all the same. Doesn't he look exactly like Tiny did at that age?" Ben scratched Tiny behind the ears as the dog thumped his foot with pleasure.

"I love him! Oh, Ben, you couldn't have gotten me a more perfect gift! Thank you!" She jumped up from the bed to give Ben a hug.

"Well, enough excitement for one day. I've got to get back to work. Take it easy, sis. I'll check back with you later, see how you're feeling."

"I'll walk you out." Roxanna left Danielle alone with the puppy.

"Good gift," Roxanna mumbled when they'd reached the front lobby doors.

"How long has she been like this?" Ben asked.

"About three weeks, since Eli left. He calls but she won't talk to him."

"Damn it. I had a feeling it was something like that." Ben cursed. "Maybe the puppy will do her some good. She looked happy to have him, right?"

"Yeah."

"I'd been planning to get her a puppy but it had to be special. When I found this little guy from the same breeder and being brother pup to Tiny…well, it was like fate."

"Puppies are cool."

"Eats a lot, poops a lot, slobbers a lot. He is a miniature version of Tiny. Hope you're up to the challenge."

"It will ease the boredom around here," Roxanna said with a straight face.

"Well, I better get going. Call me if you need anything."

"Yeah."

Roxanna watched man and dog walk out then she returned to Danielle's room.

Danielle knew she was having her nightmares regularly again but didn't know why. It was usually some trauma or stress in her life that set her off, but she couldn't put her finger on the cause of them now. Telling Roxanna or Ben would only worry them and she didn't want to ruin their Christmas, so she kept it to herself. As she'd always done in the past, she planned to deal with her problems on her own and move on. The puppy was a good start.

When she returned from her last minute Christmas shopping trip to town, she was greeted by a stampeding puppy skidding into her legs across the slippery polished marble floor of the hotel lobby.

"I hope you had time to think about puppy names because I'm getting sick of calling him Puppy." Roxanna greeted her from her usual spot at the front desk. The puppy followed Danielle with a sloppy-big-footed-slobber-dribbling lope, tripping over himself the whole way.

"Come on, Puppy. Let's go brainstorm for names." As

soon as Danielle had the door open, he rushed ahead of her into the apartment. Roxanna stood in the open doorway, watching her unpack and put away her purchases.

"What are you going to do when Eli calls again? Are you going to talk to him?"

Danielle doubted he would call. She'd dodged several, hoping he'd eventually give up. Why was he calling? And why wasn't she brave enough to just take one of his calls, just to tell him to stop calling?

Because he left her.

He stayed just long enough for her to drop her guard, become attached to him - maybe even fall for him a little bit – and then he just left. So why did he keep calling?

"No, I don't want to talk to him."

"Why not?"

"I just don't, okay?"

"Whatever. Chicken."

"Chicken? Why am I a chicken?"

"You're afraid you'll actually enjoy talking to him, start caring about a man, maybe even want him to come back." Danielle hated it when Roxanna knew how her brain worked. "And you're afraid of getting your feelings hurt if he doesn't feel the same way. Chicken."

Danielle snorted.

"What's that supposed to mean?"

"It means, you hypocrite, you've been in love with my brother for so long without doing something about it that you really have no room to lecture me about men."

"Fine. But our situations are totally different. Ben barely knows I'm alive, unlike Eli, who clearly has the hots for you."

"Time to change the subject."

"Wimp."

"Hypocrite."

"I stand by my original conviction. Chicken."

A crash from across the room was a welcome change of subject for both women, neither wanting to admit they had feelings for a man. Puppy was playing with Christmas decorations under the tree. "Any names for the puppy?" Roxanna asked after clearing her throat, an obvious move to pretend their previous conversation hadn't taken place.

"I wanted something strong. I mean, he's cute and cuddly now, but he needs a name that he'll grow into. I've narrowed it down to Gunnar, Butch, Bull, Thor, or Spike. Any of those sound good to you?" Danielle watched the puppy, imagining him growing up to be another Tiny.

"Okay, Spike."

"Spike. That was easy." They turned toward the puppy

and Danielle called him by his new name. "Spike! Here Spike…"

The puppy ignored them.

"Okay, so it's going to take some time to introduce him to the idea."

****Chapter Twenty-Three****

"Before I forget, a package came for you. Here." Roxanna pushed a small package toward Danielle on the counter, having just pulled it from that day's mountainous pile of Christmas, New Year's and Thank You greeting cards just delivered by their mailman.

"It's from Chicago."

"Yeah?"

"Yeah."

"Open it," Roxanna coaxed, nudging Danielle when she just stood staring at the mysterious unopened package. "You either open it now or I will. Here, give it to me." Roxanna reached for the package only to have Danielle pull it back, hugging it to her chest.

"Okay, okay. I'll open it." Danielle tore off the brown paper covering the package to reveal a smaller box. She ripped it open while Roxanna watched.

"This looks like jewelry. Jewelry is a very personal gift. I don't know if I can handle something personal, Rox." She stared at the unopened velvet box.

"Open it, Danni."

The box popped open with a snap of its hinges.

"It's a necklace." Nestled in the box was a tiny detailed pendant hanging from a fine silver chain. "A rosebud."

"Let me help you put it on." Roxanna lifted the delicate necklace from its box and walked around behind Danielle to hook it around her neck, brushing her hair aside then settling it back after the necklace lay in place.

"The man has fine taste in jewelry."

"Yes." Danielle said with a sniff, trying not to shed the tears gathering in each eye. "I'm not crying!"

"Whatever." Roxanna chided the other woman.

Roxanna smiled as she watched the other woman escape to the privacy of her apartment.

"She's always been stubborn."

"Damn, Ruth! Don't you know better than to sneak up on a person like that?"

"Sorry, you must not have noticed us standing here the

whole time. Fancy that, sister. They don't even notice us anymore."

"Pfft!" Roxanna sputtered. "We just kind of had something important going on." She stopped dusting and tucked the supplies under the desk, all under the watchful eye of Sebastian. Her fingers reached for the calming influence of the big yellow cat, scratching her fingers through his thick fur while his tail flicked. His purr machine vibrated from his barrel chest while a smile spread across his face, eyes closed.

"Yes, we saw." Edna replied. The two sisters stood, as usual, side by side facing Roxanna over the counter. "Did her young man send her that beautiful necklace?"

"Yeah."

"Yes sir, she is a stubborn one."

"Always has been…"

The sound of a vehicle pulling up in front of the hotel silenced them. Ruth and Edna disappeared as Roxanna went to the front windows. A black Ford Expedition with dark tinted windows parked at the far end of the driveway and the driver, bundled up in a warm winter coat pulled high up around his neck, climbed out.

Roxanna hoped it wasn't a last minute guest looking for a room. There weren't any rooms available at the hotel, and she couldn't be sure there would be any at the B&B in town either. The hotel was booked up solid until after New Years.

The man blew into the lobby, the front doors slamming shut behind him as the winter wind fought to follow him indoors. Stomping his feet on the rug, he took his time crossing the lobby before facing her across the front desk.

"Hi, Roxie. Merry Christmas…a little late." Unbuttoning his coat and draping it over one arm, he shook the fresh snow from his head and shoulders.

"Eli. To what do we owe this unexpected visit?" she asked, watching him comb the snow from his hair but wasn't sure what temperature of greeting she was willing to give him…yet. "I hope you weren't planning to get a room because we are booked up solid until after New Years."

"No, no. I'm fine. Is Danielle around?"

"In her apartment."

"Roxie, I think we need to…" Danielle's door swung open as she burst into the lobby, crashing to a halt when she spotted the man at the front desk with Roxanna. "Eli…" Her hand went to her throat, grasping the necklace nestled against her skin.

"Danielle." They eyed each other from across the room. "You wouldn't take any of my calls."

"No."

"Can we, please, go somewhere and talk?"

"Yeah. That's a great idea," Roxanna said. The room pulsed and the tension building between the two was making her uncomfortable. "Why don't you two kids go talk in Danni's apartment. In private." With a firm grip on each, she marched the two toward the open doorway of Danielle's apartment and shoved them in, slamming the door behind them. "And don't come out until you've had that good long talk."

"It's about time." Ruth said beside her.

"Geez! Would you quit popping in and out on me!" Roxanna exclaimed.

"Sorry."

"Do you want something warm to drink?" Danielle asked Eli. "Some hot chocolate maybe?"

"Sounds good, it was a long drive here. Looks like we have a nasty snow storm picking up out there." After tossing his coat over the back of the sofa, he joined her in the kitchen but leaned back on the opposite counter when she shied away from him.

"Yes, bad snow storm. Lots of snow. Very cold." He noticed her hands shaking as she was mixing the hot chocolate. That was a good sign. She was nervous. There may be hope for them yet.

"Danielle…"

"What?"

"Danielle, how have you been?"

"What?"

"We're supposed to be talking."

"What did you want to talk about?" She started to turn away from him but he caught her by one arm and swung her around to face him, holding her by both arms.

"I know you're angry because I left to go back to Chicago. I get that. But I'm here now, I took care of my business and got back as soon as I could."

"No."

"Come here, I need to hold you." He leaned back against the counter and pulled her into him. Running his tongue across her neck, he tasted her, breathing in the scent that was Danielle, the silky texture of her skin. Would he ever get enough of this woman? Could he?

"Eli…"

"I'm right here." On his tongue, he felt the vibration in her neck as she whispered his name.

"…I was perfectly fine without you…" He smiled at the catch in her breath when he nipped at her chin for lying.

His lips traveled down her neck then stopped when he encountered the chain nestled there.

"So, you got my gift. When I saw it, I remembered that day in the rose bushes. The first time we kissed." He leaned away from her to study her face. She was nervous, but what he focused on was her body's response to him. He could smell it, taste it, feel it. She wanted him, she was just too stubborn to admit it. "You look like you haven't been sleeping well. Have you been having your nightmares again?"

"I'll be okay."

"Danielle, how long have you been like this?"

Her whole body stiffening, she poked that stubborn chin out at him. "I'm fine. Now, I want you to leave."

"Have you seen a doctor? Does Ben know you've been sick?"

"I'm not sick. Please leave."

"Tsk tsk, Danielle," he clucked his tongue at her, amused by her stubbornness. "I'm not going anywhere. This is how things are going to go. We are going to get married, as soon as possible."

"Are you crazy? What are you talking about?"

"You are clearly in love with me."

"You're pretty full of yourself aren't you?" She still

wouldn't meet his eyes, maybe that was a good sign. Maybe she needed him to prove he wasn't going to leave her again.

"Not so much, but I am pretty sure of you and I know you wouldn't have made love with me if you didn't have feelings for me."

"It was just sex and you're wrong. It's time for you to leave. " She swung around and headed down the hall to her bedroom. Following her seemed like the right thing to do. He wasn't done talking yet, and this was just starting to get fun.

"I came back...does that count for anything? After we're married, we'll have to work on that stubborn streak of yours."

"I. Am. Not. Marrying. You." She stabbed the words at him.

"Yes. You. Are." He stabbed back.

He saw her hands clench into fists and he took a step away from her.

"Now, now, Danielle. You don't want to be hitting your future husband, how would you explain that in our wedding pictures when I have a bruise on my face...I mean another bruise...hmmm? And, that hurt, by the way, so please don't do that anymore."

"You're impossible! Get out of my room!" Grabbing a pillow from the bed, she hit him with it before he could jump out of the way. He wasn't expecting that.

"Temper temper. I think I'll go keep Roxie company while you think it over. At least she'll act like she's happy to see me." Spinning on his heel, he left the room.

"Infuriating man…" she muttered, loud enough for him to hear from the hallway.

Infuriating woman…

Letting himself out of her apartment, he was hit in the shins by an excited puppy, nearly knocking him off his feet and driving him up against the wall.

"Spike! Bad boy, sorry." Roxanna dragged the puppy off him and backed away to face Eli.

"Who is this?"

"Spike, meet Eli." By way of introductions, Roxanna lifted the puppy's front paw to Eli.

"I noticed Danielle is looking tired and thinner than usual. Has she seen a doctor?"

"Ask her." Roxanna walked away from Eli with Spike trailing behind her, Eli followed, not sure what else to do.

"I have plenty of time to get the answers, I guess. I can be an incredibly patient man." He flashed Roxanna a confident smile and leaned forward on the front counter, prepared to charm her for the answers he wanted.

"Whatever." Roxie mumbled.

Note to self: Goth women weren't easily charmed.

His thoughts were interrupted as Ben entered the lobby then stopped when he spotted Eli. The thunderclouds forming on his face were not lost on Eli.

"Hey, Ben."

"Eli. If I'd known you were going to be here, I would have brought my cuffs and gun. Wait here, I can still go get them from my car."

"Uh, oh. So, you're mad at me too?"

"Mad? Mad? That doesn't even begin to cover it!" Ben's voice blasted across the deserted lobby. "How many times did I tell you to keep your hands off my sister? Huh? How many times?"

"Okay, I can see you're mad..."

"I should arrest you right here and now! There are so many things I can charge you with, you won't be out of jail until your unborn children are in college!"

"Unborn children? What are you talking about? I understand you're upset. Sure, I was with your sister..."

"You're damn right I'm upset!"

"Ben. Calm down." Roxanna tried to interrupt the angry grizzly bear.

"Ben Jacobs! You stop this right now!" Danielle exploded out of her apartment and crossed the lobby in bare feet to join them. "What is going on out here? And it had better not be some male-chest-thumping I'll-show-you-mine-if-you-show-me-yours challenge. I've had all I can take of men and their caveman egos! I have guests staying here, trying to relax and enjoy themselves and you two are having a pissing match in my front lobby?" She had changed into jeans and a baggy sweatshirt, not bothering with shoes or socks, but Eli thought she looked sexy as hell. He couldn't stop his eyes from wandering over her, remembering every inch but especially enjoying those bare toes.

"Take your eyes off my sister! Haven't you done enough?" Ben bellowed at him.

"Ben! That's enough!" Danielle snapped, a tightly controlled volcano threatening to erupt. Eli was fascinated that this woman could so easily control her brother, who outweighed her by fifty pounds and towered over her slender form.

"Wait a minute…what were you talking about when you said unborn children? Danielle? What was he talking about?" His heart hammering in his chest, Eli was ready to beg for answers if he had to.

"Calm down, Jackass! She's not pregnant! At least, she'd better *NOT* be! I might still arrest you yet!"

"Shut up, Ben. Everybody! Just shut up! I'm going to my room and I don't want to hear any more yelling! And nobody had better follow me! Nobody!" She disappeared into her apartment before anyone had the chance to respond, the slamming of her door echoing through the suddenly silent lobby.

"Well, that was fun!" Roxanna finally spoke as the only silent spectator to the conversation. "What do you have planned later on tonight for entertainment?"

****Chapter Twenty-Four****

Knocking on her door, he let himself in, not waiting for her to answer. He found her standing in the middle of the living room, her arms hugging her body. The stubborn set of her chin and tight white-knuckle grip she had on her arms was at odds with the trembling chin and teary eyes staring back at him.

She wanted him to see her as strong, in control, independent.

He saw the fear. She was so tightly wound, he imagined her close to shattering into a million pieces if he said the wrong thing.

"You drive me crazy sometimes, you know that?"

"Fine, just go back to where you came from. Then I won't drive you crazy anymore, problem solved."

"Stop it, Danielle! I'm not going anywhere."

"Why not? We don't need you here! I was just fine before you came along. Go back to Chicago."

"I can't."

"Why?"

"Because I no longer live in Chicago."

"What?" He ached to hold her in his arms, to reassure her.

"I live here now, well, in town anyway. Go look in my truck if you don't believe me, you'll find it full of my worldly possessions. I'm a writer, I can write anywhere and this place is good for me."

"So, you came back because you can write well here. Is that it?"

"No. That's just an added bonus. I actually came back because of a certain aggravating, strong, stubborn, smart, independent, beautiful, temptress living up here. I've found life without her just isn't the same. And if she'll have me, I'd very much like to spend the rest of my life with her." As he was talking, he slowly advanced on her, walking her backwards until she was up against the wall.

He leaned in to slide his face into her neck, catching her scent, wanting to taste her. "I have a ring here that belongs on your finger. Can we, please, put the thing where it belongs?"

"I don't know…"

"GOD WOMAN! Do you want me to beg?"

"I don't remember hearing a proposal. All I've heard is your claim that we are getting married, kinda bossy if you ask me. I've always liked to think I'm in control of my life. Then you come barging in and try to boss me around." She tried to capture his lips but he stepped away from her and dropped to one knee. Looking up into her stunned face, he opened the box, flashing the diamond.

"Danielle Jacobs. From the first moment we met, I knew my life would never be the same again. I suffered through lengthy negotiations with agents and publishers just to convince them that relocating to be near you was in my best interest and theirs. I don't even mind dodging bullets in the rose bushes as long as I could hold you, keep you safe."

"Well, when you put it that way…"

"I need you to answer a question that has been bugging me for a long time." Eli was leaning on the counter of the front desk, Danielle beside him. They had just shared their good news with Roxanna, when he changed the subject.

"O-kay." No question he had to ask her was going to

shake her up, especially since his most recent question ended with her happily answering with a yes. "What do you want to know?"

"What is it with this front counter anyway? I mean, sometimes I'd swear something died back there, the smell is unbearable. Then other times, it starts vibrating for no reason. What is up with that?"

Danielle shared a secret smile with Roxanna and dropped her hand to the counter top, realizing she'd been scratching Sebastian behind the ears. His purr was a deafening roar to her ears, and the ear-to-ear grin on his face an accurate portrait of how she felt.

∎∎∎

Malynda McCarrick was born and has always lived in Iowa and wouldn't dream of living anywhere else.

A country girl at heart, she's always lived with animals - horses, cattle, cats, dogs, geese and the occasional pets of spiders and snakes - and incorporates them in most of the artwork and stories she creates. Another vital element in her work is humor and a firm belief that if you aren't enjoying yourself at any project, it's time to move on. Life is meant to be enjoyed, not simply endured.

Malynda loves to hear from her fans and readers.

You can reach her at malyndamccarrick@gmail.com or visit her website at malyndamccarrick@com where you can learn more about future stories and events.

Made in the USA
Charleston, SC
02 March 2011